LAST CHANCE CHRISTMAS

Last Chance Christmas

MICHAEL J. MOORE

Dedicated to all my Beta readers:

Marion

Libby

Patti

Rudi

Stacey

Thanks for all your helpful feedback!

And a special THANK YOU to my friend Mouna, for inspiring this story.

Other titles available from Michael J. Moore:

Robert Lowe: An Origin Story
The Tales Of Robert Lowe

A Cowboy Christmas

www.MichaelJMooreAuthor.com

Cover design and art by Britton Mitchell

Prologue - Part One

"Don't look now but here he comes." As her best friend said the words, a shiver ran down her spine. She wasn't sure if it was because she thought he was so cute or because she was afraid he would throw some smart-ass comment her way. She was fairly certain he didn't look at her the same way she looked at him. She wasn't exactly the height of late 90's fashion with her frizzy hair, thick glasses and braces on her teeth. She knew she wasn't his type, whatever that was. But a girl could hope. And while she hoped, she braced herself for the worst.

"Don't look now but it looks like four-eyes stuck her finger in an electric socket!" He said it to no one in particular but his best friend, who seemed to be stuck to his side like glue, could always be counted on to provide the obligatory feedback in the form of an uproarious laugh, even if what was said was rarely funny to anyone but the two of them.

She seldom spoke back to him but decided that day she wasn't going to be a doormat for him to stomp on any longer. "Well, aren't you original?"

"She speaks!" he chided back.

"Yes, I do. And in full sentences that make sense, which is more than I can say for either of you two." She started to dig in her heels, not sure why she suddenly felt like fighting back, so to speak. "And if you're going to make fun of someone, at least put some effort into it."

"No need," he retorted. "All I need to do is hold up a mirror to your face and I don't need to say another word." His best friend snickered loudly.

"Believe me, it would be refreshing for all of us if you didn't say another word. But at least you came up with something clever to say. Guess you haven't smoked enough weed today to cloud up your head. But it's early, especially for you."

Just as her best friend was about to suggest they get to class, the bell rang. "And now you've made us late!" The two girls started running down the hall. His friend followed them.

"Don't worry goodie two-shoes," he called after her. The teacher would never report you for being late!" He watched as she disappeared around a corner, then turned to head somewhere, most likely not to a classroom. But standing in front of him was the vice-principle. *Damn!* he thought. *Looks like another detention for me.* He knew his father would not be happy.

But then, he never was.

Prologue - Part Two

She looked out the window with a tear in her eye as she watched her uncle back out of the driveway. This wasn't how she had pictured the evening. Her father and his brother always had a strained relationship but now that she was 15, she thought it was time to put the family back together. She had rehearsed the evening over and over in her head. She knew what she would say to spark respectable conversation between the two of them. She just knew it would go smoothly. Wiser than her years, she wasn't quite wise enough to realize that some things might not be "fixable".

The evening had started off well, with her father and uncle catching up. Her father talked about how well his business was doing, that he had a poker group which played regularly and his project remodeling the basement of his house was proceeding nicely. After dinner, he finally asked his brother how his life was going.

Her uncle being a Washington Nationals fan, he was happy to recount the memorable plays from the World Series the team had just won and then talk about his new job. "We're helping a lot of people," he stated proudly.

That's when everything started to go south. Her father couldn't resist teasing his brother about the fact that he "could have used some of that help" when they were younger. Her uncle let the comment slide but when her father kept inserting little digs into the conversation about the family's troubled past, she could see her uncle was tiring of being reminded how their youthful years were robbed from them by issues that were not of their making…at least initially.

She knew that her family had a checkered past that she didn't understand when she was younger. But now that she was older, she enjoyed spending time with her uncle and never understood why her father didn't get along with his younger brother. He was fun and funny and nothing like her father. She wanted all of them to spend more time together. They were the only family each of them had.

The one thing she remembered her mother saying as she was walking out the door for the last time was, "Don't ever forget the importance of family." She never really understood the statement. Being only 8 years old when her mother left, she wondered if family was so important, why did her mother leave? She realized not long after that, while family might be important, her mother had other plans to build another family with someone else. She wondered why her mother didn't take her along.

"Because she's a selfish…" Her father would never finish the statement he often started.

Before long, she came to realize that her mother left because she simply couldn't handle the stress her father imposed on their life together. And he would have made his soon-to-be ex-wife's life miserable if she had taken their only child with her. If she left child behind, she would have no reason to be in contact with her soon-to-be ex-husband.

With her uncle's taillights long gone, she turned to her father. "Why do you always have to ride him like that?" she asked as he cracked a beer and plopped down in his chair. She was angry at her father for making his brother feel like he had failed in life.

"He needs a dose of reality sometimes. Helps build character." He always felt his younger brother never would have made it out of his teens without him there as their father weaved his web of nefarious complexities that affected them all, often abruptly and without warning, at least none that the two brother's could see.

"Or maybe you could just appreciate what he's accomplished, especially after what he's gone through." She knew reasoning with her father was futile but she tried as often as she could. "He came here to try and have a nice evening with us and after boasting about all the things that are going right for you, you barely acknowledged that he has a life. And when you finally asked what's he's doing, you started tearing it down. What's wrong with you?" She knew she was treading on thin ice but she didn't know any other way to make her point.

"Look, you don't know what our life was like when we were younger. I don't talk about it but it wasn't good. Our father wasn't a good man and he made our lives...very difficult."

Like father like son she thought to herself but dared not speak the words.

"And your uncle managed to make things even worse for himself. I tried to keep him on the straight and narrow but he was determined to do whatever he wanted whenever he wanted, regardless of the consequences."

"But he straightened himself out and now he's helping others."

He gave her a dismissive wave of his hand and huffed. "He thinks he's helping others when he should be helping me with my business. Which I doubt he could do anyway so it's best he stays out of my way."

"And that attitude is the very reason why he will gladly stay out of your way. But I want him around." She put her hands on her hips and glared at him as he guzzled his beer. "He's family and that's supposed to be important. He's all we have."

He looked at his daughter. She lectured him the same way her mother did. And he didn't miss her lecturing so he wasn't about to let his daughter take up the same annoying habit. "I suggest you watch your tone with me little missy. There are a lot of things you don't know, even though you think you know everything. He's a loser and won't ever be anything else." He took a long pull on his beer, his 8th of the day. "Don't forget that I went through all that crap too. We *both* came through it all."

"You know he went through a lot more afterwards, not that it was a competition."

"Why are you always defending him?" His voice started to rise. "He made choices and suffered the consequences of those choices, just like me."

She rolled her eyes. "Oh yeah, go ahead and remind me again that I was "the surprise you never wanted" and blame me *again* for mom leaving."

"You said it, not me", he sneered as he took another swig.

"Just figured I'd save you the trouble," she spit back. "She certainly wouldn't have left because of your warm personality."

He glared at her as he remained silent.

"But don't worry, I'll be out of your hair soon enough."

He almost spat out the beer he just swigged. "Oh yeah, listen to the little girl spouting off about her big plans. You know as well as I do I'm stuck with you for a long, long time."

"You wish!" She shot him a menacing look. "There is no way I'm staying here past my 18th birthday. And when you're sitting here trying to figure out how to turn the oven on so you can cook your dinner that will no doubt come frozen in a box, maybe you'll finally regret how you treated the only daughter you'll ever have, God willing."

"You better watch your tongue little lady. You think you're so mature but you don't know how to do much other than cook and clean. Don't think you're gonna do any better than what you got right now!"

She laughed at her father's declaration. It was a joke to her that he actually believed the drivel that came out of his mouth. "You can't stand the thought that someone in this family could accomplish something. But it sounds like he's really doing some good things over there."

"I guess it takes a delinquent to help another delinquent," he snorted.

"Doesn't matter how he started out," she noted. "What matters is that he's doing good now. And soon as I can get outta here, I will too!"

"Yeah, you keep dreaming." Another swig of beer.

"Yeah, I have dreams. The biggest is to get away from you."

He held his beer up. "Good luck to you."

"You think I can't do it but I've been studying about animals in school and putting what I'm learning to use at the ranch."

"That's why you spend so much time there. I figured you were out with some boy, doing what your mother did best." He raised his eyebrows with an expression that sickened her.

"You would think that, since that's all you think anyone ever thinks about. You really are disgusting."

"I'm not telling you again to watch your mouth."

She laughed. "Like you're in any condition to do anything about it. You're already so drunk that if you managed to struggle out of your chair, you'd face-plant after two steps."

She couldn't stand talking to him any longer. She went to the kitchen and started putting away the leftovers and cleaning up the dishes. She wasn't quiet about it either. He turned up the TV volume but quickly tired of the TV blasting at him.

"Can you keep it down in there?" he shouted. "I can't hear the play-by-play on the game!"

"You can see what's happening. You need someone to explain it to you?"

Damn if she doesn't sound like her mother he thought.

When she was finally done in the kitchen, she walked into the living room and shook her head at him. "I'm going to bed before you do anything else to ruin tonight." She turned and made a beeline for her bedroom.

And locked the door behind her.

Chapter One

Much to her dismay, Judge Cooper's courtroom was busy. Very busy! Her bailiff had told her Thanksgiving Eve was going to be a light day. But it wasn't turning out that way since she had to take on cases from another court after one of her fellow judges decided to start his holiday early without bothering to notify anyone. Most of his cases could be continued but a few made their way into her court. Still, the day was moving along at a reasonable rate and she felt certain she would be able to get on the road to her sister's house by 6:00 so she could start enjoying a long holiday weekend during which she wouldn't have to worry about dishing out justice; only her famous stuffing. Well, at least it was famous within her family.

"Next case, the people vs. Jessie Thomas." Hearing the bailiff addressing the room of people brought Judge Cooper back to her current reality inside the wood paneled courtroom. The dark color of the room matched her increasingly dark mood as she watched Jessie Thomas and his lawyer William Olsson make their way to the defendant's table. She recognized the teenager and quickly referred to the file folder the bailiff had handed her, refreshing her memory with the details of the various incidents which had brought young Jessie before her several times previously. Obviously, he wasn't learning his lesson. Sometimes she wondered if she was making a difference at all in the lives of the people who traversed through her courtroom daily.

"What are the charges this time?" Judge Cooper asked the bailiff as she closed the folder.

"Stealing a car to go for a joyride," her bailiff Joe responded with eyes that reflected what the judge had been thinking. *When will these kids learn?*

The judge accepted the paper Joe handed her and read over the details of the case. She was relieved to see the car was found undamaged only a few hours after disappearing. She looked up as Jessie's lawyer anxiously awaited the start of the proceedings while Jessie himself didn't seem at all concerned with his situation. But at least the teenager was dressed as though he cared. She was used to seeing teens wearing jeans with holes in them and t-shirts with questionable artwork on the front. But as far as she could recall, Jessie Thomas had always appeared before her wearing a suit and tie. Obviously he had someone in his life pointing him in a positive direction. But it clearly wasn't enough.

"Mr. Olsson, I see from the court filings that an agreement has been reached with the wronged party in this case so we are basically here to determine the penalty Mr. Thomas should receive from this court since he has appeared here several times already and was warned his next trip through these hallowed halls would not go unpunished." Judge Cooper shot Jessie her most disappointed glare. "So I assume you are ready to tell me why I should go easy on him...again." She made no effort to hide her dismay that young Mr. Thomas was, once again, in her courtroom.

Jessie's lawyer swallowed as he held his tongue. He wanted very much to say he thought the judge had been unfair when she made her "threat" the last time Jessie appeared in court. Unfortunately, it appeared her words were more than a threat and about to come to fruition. He simply nodded.

"OK, let's hear it," said the judge as she folded her arms and rested them on the bench.

William Olsson was an up-and-coming attorney who was making his name known within the court system. Fortunately, in a good way. He was always prepared and always respectful. And always had something up his sleeve. As he carefully explained the details of Jessie's latest escapade, Judge Cooper listened while intently studying Jessie. He sat still and quiet but seemed disengaged, as if he didn't care what was going on. She knew he was intelligent as she was already familiar with his school grades from his previous appearances. But she noted as she looked through his updated file that recently his grades were slipping.

Jessie's lawyer had cleverly included a copy of his IQ test in the up-dated file which informed her that his score was impressively high.

Seated a couple rows behind the lawyer's table where her son was sitting, Kelsie Thomas was more anxious than she had ever been in her life. Nothing had prepared her for what she was going through at that moment. And life had thrown a lot her way in the preceding two years. But not knowing what was going to happen with her son was tearing her apart. She prayed William's plan would work.

As William wrapped up his summation of an action he hoped Judge Cooper would find acceptable, she heard him mention commu-nity service. *Very uninspired,* she thought. Jessie had done community service previously…more than once…so obviously that was not mak-ing the appropriate impression. Then the judge perked up when an admission was put forth that perhaps something more "intense" than community service was appropriate in Jessie's case. *Very clever,* she thought. It was William's way of letting her know that he felt as she did; community service as a punishment was not the answer.

Judge Cooper peered over the top of her reading glasses as she ad-dressed Jessie's lawyer. "I feel certain that you are not suggesting jail time for your client Mr. Olsson, so what do you have in mind?"

"Well your honor," William responded, "as you know, there are several court-approved programs for troubled youth in this state and I feel that Jessie might benefit from one of them."

Jessie started to appear slightly anxious as he sat in the sturdy wooden chair next to his lawyer.

From his demeanor, the judge was having trouble gauging Jessie's frame of mind regarding what his lawyer had suggested. "Mr. Thomas, do you have anything to say before I consider Mr. Olsson's recommendation?"

Jessie didn't look up from the void at which he was staring as he shrugged. William gave him a swift nudge in the leg as he glared down at his young client. When Jessie looked up with an expression of *What the hell did you kick me for?* and saw William's agitated expres-sion shooting back at him, he knew he needed to straighten up his attitude, whether he meant it or not. The lawyer had warned him not to be insolent during the proceedings as a disrespectful attitude was all the judge would need to justify locking him away. He sat up a bit in his chair and muttered. "No, your honor."

The judge addressed Jessie firmly. "Young man, I'm not sure you understand the gravity of your situation. In the last year, you have appeared before me several times. And each time you are here, the situation is dire. If you don't straighten out your act, you will...and notice I didn't say *might*...end up behind bars. In fact, I can make that happen today if I don't see any other appropriate course of action. You may think that you can do whatever you want because you are from a certain neighborhood or class of people but I can assure you of one thing. In my courtroom, where you live and where you come from matters to me not one iota. So trust me when I tell you that you are not entitled in here. If I feel there is no chance that you will change your ways, you leave me no choice. And I'm not seeing that you want to make a change." Judge Cooper was starting to feel exasperated. "Has it been explained to you exactly what could actually happen to you today?"

Kelsie could contain herself no longer. Sitting in the courtroom gallery, watching the judge as she decided the fate of her son and hearing the harsh reality of the situation spoken out loud, she couldn't stop herself as she sprang from her seat. "Believe me, I have your honor!" She blurted out the words as William's warning that she should not speak in court blasted in her head.

The judge looked in Kelsie's direction, finding her in the middle of a row of seats. "Mrs. Thomas, I didn't see you there. Almost thought you had missed your son's latest court date."

"I'm sorry to interrupt your honor, but I want to assure you that Jessie and I have had several conversations about his situation and even though it may not appear so, he has a clear understanding of what could happen today."

Judge Cooper wasn't impressed. "You're correct. It doesn't appear to me at all that Jessie has given much consideration to exactly what might happen here today."

"If I may, your honor," Kelsie continued. "I believe you are aware of the recent change in our situation so I'm begging you to please consider giving Jessie one last chance to turn things around. As you know, he's all I have and I know he is a better person than his recent actions reflect." Kelsie was suddenly aware of all the eyes in the room that were upon her and the ears that went along with them. She was normally a reserved individual but at that moment, she didn't care if she had to beg for her son to remain out of jail in front of others. She would do whatever it took for her to get her son back.

Judge Cooper sat silent and still, alternately studying Jessie and his mother. She didn't have children of her own but she had adjudicated many cases that had a serious affect on many families over the years. Far too many in her mind. And she knew that in many of the cases where she handed down severe penalties, they were penalties that were well-deserved. But even without experiencing motherly intuition first-hand, she sometimes had a feeling that dissuaded her from handing down a harsh penalty when another option was available. In Jessie's case, a less-severe option was, indeed, available. And something told her it was the right path on which to send the young man, before it truly was too late.

After several moments, William spoke. "If your honor would like to take time to consider the programs I've mentioned and postpone sentencing...." He left the end of his statement unsaid, so as not to overstep his bounds, which he knew he was dangerously close to doing.

Very clever, the judge thought, knowing Mr. Olsson knew full well that with the Thanksgiving holiday coming up, postponing sentencing would give Jessie and his mother the holiday together and possibly see them through into the new year since a delay would lead to the inevitable likely not transpiring until sometime in January.

"No need, I've made my decision." Judge Cooper placed her folded hands on the bench and addressed William and Jessie. "I like your idea Mr. Olsson. I am well aware of the programs you mentioned and I'm willing to give your client the opportunity to straighten himself out in one of them."

She looked towards Kelsie and continued. "Mrs. Thomas, the bailiff will give you a website to go to where you can learn about the programs Mr. Olsson mentioned. Since you know your son better than any of us, you will likely be able to select the program in which he will have the best chance of success since clearly that is what you most desire. And believe it or not, it's what I desire as well. I expect an e-mail to be in my inbox Monday morning by 10 AM letting me know what program you have chosen for Jessie. All of them are 30 day programs so..." She paused as she looked at the calendar of cases her bailiff Joe updated every morning and placed on her bench. "It appears that we will all be back here on Christmas Eve. At that time, I will listen to the recommendation of the program administrator and decide on the final action to be taken regarding Jessie's future."

The judge paused and looked at Jessie, addressing him directly and clearly so there could be no misunderstanding. "Young man, I strongly suggest that you take this opportunity to re-evaluate your life-choices and find a better path as this is truly your last chance with me."

Judge Cooper authoritatively swung down her gavel. The snap of wood colliding with wood rang throughout the room as she called for the next case while Jessie's situation continued to play out in her mind. She felt satisfied with her decision but knew the outcome was anything but certain. She sometimes saw teenagers come out of these programs not in much better shape than when they went in. But she had seen enough come out better for the experience that she felt it made sense to give Jessie Thomas the opportunity to do the same.

She sensed something in Jessie. Even though he had barely uttered a word during his most recent court session, he had spoken more in previous appearances. She noted today that he seemed withdrawn. Clearly his home situation was having a dire affect on him and it seemed to be making him progressively worse. She had seen it all before. Sometimes the troubled teens that appeared before her simply needed a gentle push in the right direction. And sometimes they needed someone to shove them into reality. Often the youth who appeared in her courtroom were simply confused. To Judge Cooper, life seemed to get more and more complicated for young people as they endured on-line bullying, peer-pressure from all angles and the jumble of mixed messages they encountered on social media as they tried to navigate their way through life, often with only one strong adult figure in their lives. She truly hoped that this opportunity might provide just the spark to straighten Jessie out.

***

Outside the courtroom, William took the opportunity to advise his young client and his mother. "I hope you take this opportunity for the early Christmas gift that it is! The judge had no real reason to allow you to enroll in one of these programs so please understand this is a way to stay out of jail." William stared at Jessie, looking for a hint that he was concerned about his situation. Unfortunately, it appeared Jessie didn't really care and William couldn't figure out why. "Jessie, you need to take this seriously. If you don't, you could actually end up in jail."

A look flashed over Jessie's face. There it was! The concern William was hoping for, concern which informed him that his client might actually understand…or care…about what was happening. But just as quickly as he saw it, the concerned expression dissipated

Kelsie looked at her only son with despair in her eyes. "Jessie, do you understand what William is telling you? It could easily have been that you are on your way to juvenile hall or a detention center or worse right now instead of standing here with us."

For another brief moment, reality was reflected in Jessie's eyes. But in an instant, it was gone, replaced by a distant, disconnected stare. Jessie simply shrugged.

Before Kelsie let her frustration get the better of her, she addressed an equally concerned William. "Don't worry. Jessie and I will be having a serious conversation about all of this tonight."

"I hope so," William replied while continuing to stare at Jessie. "And let me know your decision regarding the program Jessie will be entering no later than Sunday morning so I can let the judge know. These programs accept participants 24/7 so as soon as you make a decision, contact them so you can get Jessie to wherever he needs to be. The sooner you get him there, the sooner he can, hopefully, come home."

Kelsie nodded in acknowledgement as she and Jessie turned to leave. Her embarrassment grew with every encounter she had with William. Jessie never displayed any concern when the lawyer was around. She figured he had already developed an opinion of her and her parenting skills that was most certainly not complimentary. And why should it be? Jessie made it seem as though he never had any type of discipline in his life, which she knew wasn't the case. She knew he had been raised properly, to respect others and do the right thing. But lately he hadn't been himself. The cause was obvious to anyone familiar with their situation; she just didn't know what to do about it. And while she didn't want Jessie to go through a program for troubled teens, he clearly needed to do just that since he never seemed to care about doing anything to alleviate his situation on his own.

As they exited the building, the gray day perfectly fit Kelsie's mood. Threatening skies followed them on their drive home, which was quiet as she didn't want to get into an involved discussion while trying to dodge the potential pitfalls of pre-holiday traffic. With the city bustling as its citizens did last minute errands before Thanksgiving, drivers seemed to be more impatient than ever. She wondered to herself why people seemed to drive more and more aggressively these days. Ever since the COVID situation, driving had become a more and more scary proposition. Tailgating, cutting in and out of traffic, speeds 20 and 30 MPH over the limit were now all too commonplace. She wondered why people couldn't seem to realize that these habits only put their lives in danger and rarely resulted in anyone actually getting to their destination any sooner, since most times the people who passed her at ridiculous speeds only succeeded in getting to the red light before her. And whenever she saw someone being irresponsible as they drove down the road, she couldn't help but pray that when the accident they would eventually be involved in happened, they didn't injure anyone but themselves. Driving was no longer something she enjoyed but she was thankful she didn't have to do it as much anymore. Working from home most days and her office being only 10 minutes from her house in the suburbs, she mercifully didn't have to spend much time on the roads.

She worried about how Jessie would be once he started taking driving lessons. At 17, he was already old enough to have a driver's license and since he was typically a responsible young man, if things had remained on track, he would already be driving. But since things had drastically changed for them both 18 months prior, she was becoming less and less confident in his ability to act rationally while managing the immense responsibility that driving imposed so she had delayed the start of his driving lessons, even though he already instinctively knew how to operate a car, as his most recent antics proved.

For something like driving lessons, his father would have been the one to direct Jessie in such matters. And he would have taught him about being a responsible driver no matter what others were doing. But with him no longer in their lives, that responsibility fell to Kelsie. And so far, she was failing in her ability to take over where her husband had previously taken the lead.

When they arrived at their 2 story, stone front, suburban home, Kelsie was barely able to pull the car into the driveway and come to a stop before Jessie quickly made a move to exit the vehicle. But she was quicker, pushing the button to lock the door.

"Before you go off to your room to sulk, I want you to know that we will be sitting down tonight to thoroughly discuss today and what program you'll be attending."

The stern tone in his mother's voice let Jessie know she was serious. And for the first time, he felt embarrassed about the situation in which he found himself. He wasn't exactly sure how it all happened.

His thoughts always seemed to be scrambled these days and he didn't know how to straighten them out. His father had always helped him figure out a way to make sense of things when life seemed to be a little too much to handle.

Jessie finally looked at his mother with true sadness in his eyes. "You pick one. It doesn't matter to me." His expression changed to one of confusion and despair, then just as quickly, it changed back to the look she had seen consistently in his eyes for far too long. Eighteen months to be exact. His hand moved to unlock the car door and he got out quickly, before she could say anything in response.

Kelsie noticed raindrops starting to appear on the windshield of the car as she watched Jessie enter the house where he could disappear into his own world, a world that included her less and less. It didn't seem like the day was going to get better anytime soon. She sat for several moments, breathing steadily. Her thoughts were running wild as she prayed for an end to their nightmare.

It took a while but as she calmed her thoughts, they turned to her husband. *Damn it Steve,* she thought to herself. *Why did you have to leave us to go through all this?* Then she chastised herself for her selfish thought. It's not like he had wanted to leave them alone. She hated that some things were beyond her control.

Chapter Two

For Kelsie, Thanksgiving Day was a bit brighter. The weather had cleared and the previous day's rain left freshness in the air that she greatly appreciated on her morning walk. She prided herself on keeping fit. And even with everything that had happened and continued to happen, she didn't dare let herself get down. She felt the one thing that was keeping her from literally going crazy was her morning routine, which consisted of exercise and a brisk walk, every morning. Her husband had often said he was initially attracted to Kelsie's athletic figure but the long wavy light brown hair cascading over her shoulders and down her back quickly became his favorite feature. And when he got to know her intellect, he knew she was the "whole package" and a day never went by that he didn't compliment her appearance. She missed that.

The holiday brought smiles out on the faces of the neighbors Kelsie saw as she walked, although many of the people she would typically see in the morning were away visiting relatives for the long weekend. The temperature had turned colder so she made a mental note to have Jessie bring some wood indoors so they could enjoy a cozy fire after dinner.

She was looking forward to her parents coming to the house for Thanksgiving. Her mother had traditionally prepared the holiday feast each year but somehow Kelsie managed to convince her that she should do it this year. After carefully finalizing the menu, she made certain that the ingredients to make all of the traditional dishes were in her pantry and fridge so her mother wouldn't regret handing over the responsibility. Of course, it was a relief that her mother insisted on preparing a few of the dishes since Kelsie was certain she wasn't up to mastering her mother's cranberry salad just yet. She had tried to make it once and the results were less than tantalizing to the taste buds. In reality, it didn't turn out bad; it just wasn't as good as her mother's. Kelsie sometimes wondered if her mother, who had many of the family recipes in her head, sometimes forgot to tell her an ingredient on purpose, so as not to be shown up by her daughter. She smiled at the thought that her mother simply wasn't ready to give up control of some things just yet.

She was also looking forward to having her parents there for the day since she was certain their presence would brighten Jessie's disposition as well as her own. She wished she saw them more but since they had moved to a retirement community an hour away, her father wasn't comfortable driving the distance very often. And she couldn't blame him. With so many ways for people to be distracted these days, not to mention the aggressive drivers who thought they ruled the roads and everyone else better get out of their way, driving had ceased to be relaxing and fun, even in the laid back area that was her childhood home. And Kelsie's life was too busy to make the trek as often as she would like. So she was happy to have a holiday that allowed everyone to get together, take a breath and relax.

She had struggled to push the pending decision regarding a program for Jessie out of her head throughout the morning and figured a bustling house and lots of food prep would help her continue to do so. She reasoned that not dwelling on the situation and waiting to make the decision until the next day wouldn't hurt anything. And she desperately wanted to have a normal holiday, even if there was no way the holidays would ever be normal again.

Kelsie had been through a lot in her almost 40 years. But the last 2 years had felt like an additional 40. Every time she looked in the mirror she wondered who it was that she saw staring back at her. She had always managed to look younger than her years. She kept her long brown hair in a contemporary style and her hazel eyes always attracted attention, as did her shapely figure, which allowed her to get away with wearing styles meant for someone that was her junior by several years.

But lately, she never felt like even acknowledging any attention that was put forth towards her. To do so felt like a betrayal. She knew it wasn't; but that didn't help. She hoped one day the feeling would pass because she knew in her head that it had to. But her heart wasn't listening.

As Kelsie arrived back home to start a busy day of cooking, she called out to Jessie. "I need you to bring some wood in and prepare the fireplace."

To her surprise, he promptly appeared in the doorway with what could possibly be construed as an excited demeanor. She knew that he was looking forward to seeing his grandparents. She was thankful he liked spending time with them. He was especially close to his grandfather and they always managed to spend time off somewhere together talking to each other about who-knows-what. She was just glad he talked with someone, wishing it was her who elicited conversation from her son. Jessie had always been a happy, outgoing boy and as he grew into being a young man, Kelsie excitedly anticipated seeing what kind of man he would come to be. As he matured, the awkwardness of his youth was replaced by a confident attitude and handsome features she knew would one day see him fighting off the girls as his body transformed into a toned physic. He kept his hair a little longer than she liked but fortunately he dressed in clothing that didn't look like it had been run over by a thousand trucks.

"You thinking Grandma will be complaining about how cold you keep it around here?" Jessie's light-hearted comment, based in the fact that her mother never missed an opportunity to point out how cold she kept the house, was refreshing to Kelsie. She appreciated his sense of humor and hadn't been privy to it nearly enough lately.

She smiled. "No doubt she will. But it's already colder than it has been and the temperature is going to fall through the day so we might as well be ready."

With that, Jessie set about getting wood from their deck, placing large logs on the bottom of the wood box which sat next to the fireplace, then filling it with smaller logs. The wood box was a warm reminder of his father, who had built it when they first moved into the house. He was very handy and always tinkering with something around the house or working on a project in the garage. The sturdy box that he built, in which he cleverly carved the words 'Wood Box' on the front panel, held enough wood to provide a cozy fire through an entire evening and was used often during the cold winter months.

Once the box was full, Jessie rolled several separate sheets of newspaper, placing them strategically on the fireplace grate. Then he placed small twigs over them, all in the manner which his father had taught him as he assured his son it was a guaranteed method for starting a successful fire. Jessie was taught at a young age that, once the small sticks were burning, larger sticks could be placed until a roaring fire was soon warming the room. His father's lesson had yet to let him down.

Kelsie was thankful the process of building the fire seemed to bring her son back to his old self, even if she knew it would not last long.

***

"Jessie, you've built your Grandmother a wonderful fire. It's so toasty!" Kelsie's mother Sarah was greatly appreciating the warmth emanating from the roaring fire as she relaxed on the couch.

"Just for you, Granny." Jessie smiled as he used his favorite sarcastic term of endearment to refer to his grandmother. She actually didn't look old enough to be his grandmother so she wasn't crazy about how her grandson chose to refer to her. But she took it with the humor which he intended. She made certain she never did typically "Granny-like" things and was careful in the way she spoke so as not to give away her age. And she was thankful her looks didn't give it away either. She was petite and feisty and managed to be mature without seeming "old". Just like her husband.

Jessie liked being around both of them.

"And Kelsie, I have to commend you on a wonderful dinner. I see my apprehension about letting you host was unwarranted."

Kelsie was exhausted but smiled with pride as she sunk into her chair. She wondered how her mother had managed to prepare all the holiday dinners by herself for so many years. She smiled at the sight of her father beginning to doze off, having seated himself at the far end of the couch immediately after the clearing of the table had started.

"Thanks Mom. Couldn't have done it without your help though. And your recipes."

"Well, I couldn't let you have all the fun!" Sarah laughed. "But based on that corn casserole recipe you found, I think the dinner would have been delicious even without my old standards."

Kelsie truly appreciated her mother's praise. Sarah was a fine cook and taught Kelsie a lot about the whole process of putting a meal together, just as Jessie's father had taught him so much. As she watched the fire dancing, she reflected on how both her mother and Jessie's father had the innate ability to teach without trying. Just involving someone in a process can often be the most effective way to teach.

Jessie placed another log in the fireplace, then challenged his grandfather to a game of chess. The quest for a game woke John up fully since he was looking forward to seeing if his grandson's skills at the game of strategy had sharpened since they last played. They quickly disappeared into Jessie's room for their match.

As Kelsie watched them walking down the hallway, she was thankful that her father could relate to Jessie since she had been feeling so hopeless at it lately. She just couldn't get him to open up about anything anymore.

"How did everything go yesterday?" Sarah had been anxious to ask her daughter about Jessie's situation but didn't want to bring in up when they were all together lest she ruin the holiday for anyone.

Kelsie detailed all that had transpired in the courtroom. Sarah asked a few questions and after she received the answers she needed, sat quietly for several moments as she contemplated all that was going on with her daughter and grandson.

Finally, Sarah spoke thoughtfully. "Back in my day, they didn't have programs like the ones you've described. Parents disciplined their kids the best way they knew how and everyone moved on. Most times it worked; sometimes it didn't." She paused as she shook her head. "But these days, it seems like parents are powerless to do what is sometimes necessary to keep their kids on the straight and narrow. Anything other than talking can get them turned into the authorities."

"Well, we're definitely past talking, which I've done until I'm tired of hearing myself." The reality of what she needed to do the next day was creeping back into Kelsie's thoughts sooner than she wanted.

Sarah asked the logical question. "Have you chosen a program yet?"

Kelsie shook her head. "Tina is coming over tomorrow to help me figure out the best one since Jessie doesn't seem to have any interest in giving me his input."

Her best friend since second grade, Tina was level-headed, analytical and practical, qualities that Kelsie was lacking when it came to her son. She knew Tina would be able to analyze each program option and help her make the best decision.

"I'm glad you've asked her for help. She'll pick a good program," Sarah confirmed.

Kelsie hoped her mother was right. This was too important to get wrong.

Chapter Three

The sun rose on a crisp, clear Black Friday morning after a Thanksgiving that actually felt a bit like a celebration. Kelsie was indeed thankful that she had been able to put her current worries aside for the day as she enjoyed time with her parents and a Jessie who, for the day, seemed somewhat like his old self.

Since she had moved back to her hometown, Kelsie had traditionally met Tina for early morning bargain hunting on the biggest shopping day of the year. Then they would hit their favorite café for lunch before more shopping that hopefully saw them completing their purchasing duties for the season. Being able to shop with her best friend after years apart made it that much more fun. But even when she had to do it on her own, Christmas shopping was always something Kelsie looked forward to as she enjoyed the experience of hunting down the perfect gifts for her family. Some years she was more successful than others but the hunt generally got easier as Jessie grew older since he had thankfully grown out of the phase where the latest impossible-to-find toy had to be found. Recent Christmases had seen him satisfied with updates to his wardrobe and a new video game or two. But this year, shopping would have to wait.

The best friends had always made their excursion together fun and poked fun at the name of the day, Kelsie teasingly calling it "Tina Friday". People that didn't know the depth of their friendship were sometimes put off when Kelsie would let her nickname for the day slip in unaccustomed company. After all, a more sensitive someone who was always looking to argue could easily take offense. Tina's African roots seemed to inform people that she *should* take offense to something that could be interpreted as slanderous to her race. But Kelsie and Tina understood each other perfectly. To Kelsie, a person's background, color, religion, orientation and whatever other labels people insisted on giving to individuals simply didn't matter. To her, everyone was the same until they proved otherwise. She never judged someone until she knew them. She wished others would do the same and was thankful she found a kindred spirit when the new girl joined her second grade class. Since the day Kelsie asked Tina if she wanted to play together at recess, the two had been inseparable, instinctively understanding each was a kind-hearted soul.

This didn't mean they didn't have to suffer more than their share of hurtful remarks from bullies at school. And besides their skin color difference, they were made even easier targets by the fact that Tina was tall and athletic, with toned legs that were made for an active life, while Kelsie was short with less natural physical prowess. But Tina helped Kelsie over the years to achieve her goal of a toned figure as they made their way together through the twists and turns of puberty, school crushes and people who just generally looked at the world in a negative light. Kelsie and Tina vowed to never let those people affect their own attitudes.

So when someone took offence to their inside jokes, they both were of the opinion that people should lighten-up. Life was too short to always be looking for some new way to be offended.

As Kelsie poured herself a cup of coffee, Tina burst through the front door without so much as a knock, wearing her usual smile that lit up any room effortlessly. She called out, "Hey girl, Happy Tina Friday!"

Kelsie popped her head out of the kitchen. "Hey yourself. The coffee is ready. Hope you are too." She took another Christmas mug from her upper cabinet as Tina walked into the room.

"I should have known you'd be getting out the holiday mugs already." Tina plopped herself on one of the barstool chairs at the kitchen island, taking her coat off as she did. She liked her friend's house. Kelsie had a knack for decorating and Tina had always thought she should have gone into the interior design field. She was constantly finding unique ways to mix old with new and make it work together seamlessly. To Tina, it seemed her friend was always redoing things in her home, enabling it to always look fresh and ready for a photoshoot for an interior design website. Tina appreciated the fact that it wasn't ostentatious and always appeared up-to-date. But in the last eighteen months, Kelsie hadn't done anything new to the house. Of course, it still looked fresh and fabulous, with the white furniture providing a clean look against the soft gray walls. Dashes of color appeared sporadically throughout the abode but were generally subtle. The kitchen had been the last room to be remodeled before Kelsie's life changed and it was very much to Tina's liking. White cabinets with frosted glass doors along with a dark gray island and light gray countertops complimented each other while the stainless steel appliances completed the room's contemporary, inviting feeling. The smell of fresh coffee perfectly enhanced the setting.

"How you doin' girl?" Tina's inquiry was genuine, knowing each day was a struggle for her friend in more ways than one.

"You know my favorite season is upon us but I'm just hoping for something to celebrate this year." Kelsie was understandably somewhat somber. "After last Christmas, we need a good one. But I'm starting to lose hope."

Tina wasn't about to let her friend, who had been through so much, start spiraling down a negative rabbit hole. "Nonsense! I'm here to make sure all hope is not lost. Pour me a cup of that coffee and fire up your computer. We're gonna take the first step to getting Jessie back on the right path."

Kelsie smiled and did as instructed. She set her computer on the island and sat next to Tina as she opened it up, then typed in the website provided by the bailiff.

As they perused the list of programs that filled the screen and read the summaries, Kelsie started to feel overwhelmed. She never had a problem making tough decisions when it came to her son. But the reality had started to set in that this was likely the toughest, most important decision she'd ever have to make regarding him. His whole future could be determined by the success or failure he would experience in whatever program she chose. If she picked the wrong one, it could prove to be the final step of a downward spiral from which Jessie might never emerge.

"This isn't going to be easy, is it?" Kelsie looked at her friend as despair started to set in.

"No, it isn't. But we're going to get through this together," Tina reassured. "Look, why don't I do the initial browse myself? I can whittle the list down to a few potential programs and then we can really examine the pros and cons of each one together."

Kelsie didn't object to her taking temporary control of the process. She watched as Tina started reading through the details of each program on her own, making copious notes. After two cups of coffee, she sat back, notes in hand.

"OK, I have four programs that look like they might work for Jessie." She referred to her notes. "All but one are within an hour's drive."

Kelsie felt relief that her friend did the initial paring down. A fresh approach and perspective was sorely needed. "Let's consider the one that's over an hour away last."

Tina punched up the website for one of the programs and turned the screen towards Kelsie. "OK, so we have this one which uses military-style discipline to get the kids in line. Judging by their success rate, their methods works"

Kelsie hesitated. "I don't want him to think I'm shipping him off to a military camp or anything like that."

"Got it." Tina typed in the next website. "Here's one that focuses on nature with lots of activities to keep the kids busy and out of trouble."

"I don't want a distraction from what's really going on. I want to find out what's bothering Jessie, besides the fact that he no longer has a father in his life." Jessie's problem wasn't a deep seated mysterious issue that Kelsie couldn't figure out on her own. The root of his problems was clear. She just needed someone to help him figure out why it had led him to make such a drastic change to the way he was acting and then figure out a way to deal with whatever it was that was tearing him apart. She was certainly having no success in that endeavor.

Tina pulled up the last of the nearby programs. "OK then, this is one which uses animals to help their participants learn responsibility while they receive counseling to delve into their issues."

Upon hearing no initial objection, Tina sat straighter in her chair and read further. "It's only 45 minutes away and their success rate is really strong. In fact, it's the best in the state!" She continued to read as Kelsie considered the option.

"Jessie does love animals. He's wanted a dog for years but we couldn't have one because of Steve. I've thought about getting one now since he's no longer here but with Jessie acting less and less responsible, I didn't want to risk getting a dog, only to potentially have Jessie bail on taking care of it."

"Understandable," Tina replied, slightly distracted as she read more about the program she had suggested. "The reviews and comments on this place are all really positive. I can't find anything negative about the facility or the staff. I had no idea they reviewed places like this on Yelp!" She continued to scroll through the information, intently clicking on pages and reading the information thoroughly. Eventually, she clicked on the staff page. A shocked and disbelieving expression made its way across her face as she slumped back in the chair. Defeated, she stared at the screen. "I can't believe this!" she finally uttered

"What is it?" Kelsie sat forward, trying to get a view of what Tina was seeing.

"You'll never believe who runs this place."

Kelsie looked at her as if to say, *how could I possibly know?*

"Brice Turner!"

It took a few seconds for the name to register in Kelsie's memory. Then she looked at her friend in disbelief. "You've got to be kidding me!" she exclaimed.

"I wish I was."

"From *our* school?"

"I think so. The staff picture certainly looks like him." She turned the computer so Kelsie could clearly see the screen.

"It can't be! How could such a loser be in charge of a program to help troubled youth?"

Brice Turner had been their nemesis all through high school. Considered by most to be the chief loser in school, the only subject he excelled in was making everyone's life a living hell with his ridiculing comments and class-disrupting antics that were constantly getting him into trouble. He was generally regarded as someone with no real hope of ever contributing anything constructive to the world. But now it appeared he was running a program that was supposed to help a segment of the population that was going through a difficult period in their lives. To Kelsie and Tina, it seems unfathomable that people in need of a dependable, level-headed mentor to help them navigate tumultuous times would ever benefit from knowing Brice Turner, since he himself was unable to navigate his own mis-guided youth successfully.

"This has to be a different person!" Kelsie exclaimed, swearing to herself that her son would not be taking part in any program headed by Brice Turner, no matter how much Jessie liked animals.

Tina was already on it. Quickly searching various social media sites, she found that the person heading the program which seemed to hold promise for Jessie, in fact, went to their school for most of his high school years. The pictures she could find from 20 years prior confirmed he was the same student who provided their least favorable memory from school.

She gave Kelsie a look that confirmed her fears. But as she continued to read about their former classmate, the more her opinion softened.

"I hate to tell you this but the more I read about the facility Brice is running, the more it seems like a perfect fit for someone in Jessie's situation." Tina kept her eyes glued to the computer screen as she spoke. "The facility and their program have the best success rate in the state and, believe it or not, they have mostly 5-star reviews." She shot Kelsie a quizzical look. "I didn't even know places like this were reviewed on Yelp!"

Kelsie simply couldn't believe it. How could someone who was clearly lost during his teens help her son? She looked over Tina's shoulder to read for herself the reviews and statistics. If what she was seeing was to be believed, it seemed a perfect fit to help Jessie. Animals at the large rural facility were used to help the program participants learn discipline and dependability while daily private and group therapy sessions helped each individual learn about the issues that were pushing them to act negatively while helping identify from where their individual issues arose and how to successfully deal with them to a more positive outcome.

It sounded like the perfect facility for Jessie. She had to figure out why he was acting so out of character!

"What do you think?" Tina could see the conflict in Kelsie's eyes.

"I don't know what to think. It doesn't make sense that someone like Brice runs this place but it's hard to argue with the results, if these statistics are to be believed."

Tina couldn't put forth a viable argument. She searched her memory to dredge up something about the long forgotten person that had suddenly been thrust squarely back into their thoughts. "I didn't think he ever graduated. I was relieved he disappeared in our senior year."

"He must have completed a GED program or something," Kelsie mused. "I always figured the school system got tired of his antics and mouth, both causing more trouble than he was worth. I thought he had been expelled permanently."

Kelsie's head was swimming. How could she subject her only son to a program where Brice Turner was involved? How would he possibly get the help he needed there? But the more she read the details and reviews of the program, she realized it was just what Jessie needed. And *Redemption* seemed an appropriate name for a facility dedicated to helping young citizens get their lives back on track. But before she would leave her son there, she needed answers to questions she had regarding the person heading up the program.

Kelsie looked at Tina with an expression of defeat that informed her friend a decision had been made. She picked up the phone and punched in a number. "I guess it's time to call William."

***

Brice entered his small living space late on the day after Thanksgiving. The apartment on the grounds of the facility he managed was simple but adequate. Every one of his days was full and hectic. The long hours and his lack of social life meant that he mostly only slept there so he didn't need more spacious quarters. The bedroom, bathroom, living area and small kitchen that comprised his dwelling were sufficient to his needs and better than the living quarters of his younger years, which were never what anyone would consider "nice" or "comfortable". And his family never lived anywhere long enough that it made sense to improve their surroundings.

His time spent living in his current abode had already lasted longer than any place he had previously laid his head. The rather non-descript furnishings were functional and comfortable even if they were nothing special to behold. But the one indulgence he afforded himself was a quality set of audio equipment and a significant collection of music. It covered one wall of the living area and often provided him comfort on days when he wasn't sure he was making enough progress with those he was charged with helping.

He powered up his equipment as he settled in for the evening, thankful he didn't agree to spend the long holiday weekend at his brother's place. Every year it was the same: his only niece would convince him that the holiday was time for family to be together. But his brother's idea of "family-time" didn't differ much from their father's warped interpretation of the term, so every year Brice could only stomach being there for dinner and nothing more. And if it weren't for his niece, he wouldn't even agree to go there for dinner. But he knew his presence made it difficult for his brother to berate her incessantly so year after year, he only went for her benefit. Fortunately, every year her cooking improved until he actually looked forward to the meal. He was impressed that, at a young age, she managed to master the making of such an important meal with no mother around to guide her. His niece impressed him more and more each year. Unfortunately, he could never look forward to the company that went with the food. So, rather than drive all the way home after such a big meal, he always rented a cabin in the woods where he would stay the night after leaving his brother's home as soon as he could without hurting her feelings. He quietly harbored hope that one year, maybe, just maybe, his brother would mellow out enough that he would actually be fun to be around. If that ever happened, Brice would stay the night and maybe things could be better.

To date, he had yet to stay the night at his brother's home.

While Brice didn't think much of his brother, he loved his niece and wished he had the ability to take her out of her home situation. But with no physical abuse taking place, he had no legal basis on which to file a motion to have her removed from the home to live with him. Fortunately, she seemed to deal with the situation fairly well. He was thankful she would be turning 18 soon and therefore be able to remove herself from the situation if she wanted. He would help her if he could but the reality was, Brice had his hands full running his facility for troubled youth. But being around his brother was always a reminder of just how close he himself came to being like him. If life had taken a different turn, there would have been one more loser in a family already brimming with them. He turned that sad thought over in his head as he picked an album out of his collection by Melanie, a folk singer who was popular long before Brice was born but managed to become one of his favorite singers after he found an album of hers in his mother's small collection. He placed it on the turntable and adjusted the volume, then sat back to enjoy the music while he checked his e-mails.

He read through the status reports his staff sent every day. During the two days he had been away, it appeared nothing out of the ordinary occurred so the weekend would be fairly quiet. As he was about to close his in-box, an e-mail came through notifying him of the pending arrival on Monday of a new program participant. Since he had nothing pressing to do, he decided to look over the file attached to the e-mail to familiarize himself with the individual's details before their first meeting.

Nothing seemed unusual about the case: Single mother; no siblings; acting out since losing his father 18 months prior; needing to straighten out his life's direction or face potential jail time.

As the details regarding the incidents which led the pending program participant to Redemption's door were digested, certain aspects of the case were all too familiar to Brice...and personal. He printed out the case details and placed them in a file folder, marking it with the pending program participant's name: Jessie Thomas.

Chapter Four

The ride to Redemption early Monday morning was quiet. Kelsie was uneasy during the drive, knowing it was the least appropriate time to lecture her troubled son about what was at stake for the umpteenth time. So they mostly rode in silence. But she knew she had to say something before she left him there. And it had to be profound, something that would make an impression on him to last through the period they would be apart. She spent the entire drive trying to figure out what those words should be. Whenever she had to rally her staff on a major project, she would carefully rehearse everything she wanted…needed…to say. And as soon as she would start to speak, everything she planned to say would fall out of her head and she would end up "winging it". Sometimes it worked out; sometimes it didn't. She wanted to make sure whatever she said to Jessie wasn't something random. There was so much which needed to be said that she wasn't sure she could fit everything into a speech that didn't drone on and on.

"Mom, you know the exit's coming up, right?"

Jessie's question brought her back to the moment. She was concentrating so intently on what she wanted to say she almost missed the exit. She noted the sign for Route 32 was only a half mile away and she was still in the fast lane. Thankfully there were no cars near her so she easily moved to the right lane before it was too late.

The facility wasn't far from the exit so only minutes after leaving the highway, they were pulling up to the gate. And Kelsie was far from having her speech ironed out. She hesitated, then pushed the button below the small camera on the keypad at the gate entry. Moments later a calm voice came over the speaker.

"Hello. Welcome to Redemption. How can I help you?"

"Hi," Kelsie stated in as cheerful a voice as she could muster. "I'm Kelsie Thomas with my son Jessie. We have a 9:00 appointment."

"Yes, of course Ms. Thomas. Please enter through the gate and pull into any of the visitor spaces. My name is Grace. I'll be right down to meet you."

Jessie watched as the gate slowly opened. He felt as though he was about to panic but didn't want to show his mother he was as scared as he was. He was finally starting to realize the gravity of his situation.

Kelsie did as instructed and pulled into a space as far away from the entrance as possible, as if it would make any significant delay to the inevitable happening. She knew she only had moments to say whatever she could muster. With her thoughts still jumbled up in her head, she spoke from the heart.

"Jessie, I know it seems like we're in a dire situation but you need to realize it's going to be OK. We're going to get through this."

Jessie looked at his mother with apprehension in his eyes. "You mean *I'm* going to get through this...hopefully." He turned to look out the window at what he basically felt was a prison...*his* prison...for the next 30 days.

Kelsie stared at him in disbelief. "No, I mean *we*. We are a family and what affects you affects me. What bothers you bothers me. What happens to you happens to me."

"Well, you aren't getting dumped here. I am."

Kelsie turned in her seat to face her son. "Look, I know you don't want to believe this but you aren't getting *dumped* here. I'm bringing you here with the hope that they will be able to help you with whatever it is that's got you all turned around." She paused, knowing perfectly well the basis for Jessie behavior of late. "Besides the obvious."

Jessie stared out the car window as the woman he presumed to be Grace approached. He imagined the disembodied voice he had heard at the gate belonged to someone who would remind him of his second-grade teacher, a woman who terrified him every time she looked in his direction. But the woman approaching looked less like a strict task-master and more like someone who always had fresh baked cookies in her kitchen. Her kind face was in total contradiction to what he had been imagining everyone at his home for the next 30 days would be like. He couldn't quite reconcile his imagination to his reality as he felt his emotions rising to the surface while struggling to keep them under control. *Boys don't cry* he told himself more and more these days.

Kelsie rushed to complete her thoughts before she no longer had the opportunity. "It may seem like its too late but I hope you know that you can talk to me about anything, *anything* that is bothering you! I know you used to do that with your father and I could never take his place but I *am* your mother. I'll never judge you and I'll always listen. I want to make sure you know that. But if you won't, or can't, talk to me, please talk to the counselors here. They are trained to help you."

Jessie removed his seatbelt and opened the door as he mumbled, "Got it."

Damn it! Kelsie scolded herself. *That's not what I wanted to say.* But the moment had passed and Jessie was out of the car and Grace was there and it was suddenly time to get it over with. She exited the car as Grace reached her, hand extended.

"Hi Kelsie, I'm Grace. Very nice to meet you."

They shook hands as Kelsie responded. "Hi Grace, nice to meet you as well. This is my son Jessie."

Jessie looked at Grace briefly before turning his stare towards the barn and stable in the distance. The buildings were the standard red color he'd seen in so many movies and pictures of farms. They were large and bustling with activity. He could see several people his age buzzing around, accomplishing various tasks while several adults appeared to be supervising.

Inmates and wardens he thought to himself.

The large building at the end of the parking area from whence Grace had approached seemed to be the central facility and he could see several dorm-style buildings behind it. The cloudy skies and cold weather did nothing to boost Jessie's spirits as reality set in. He listened as Grace and his mother talked.

"Jessie's counselor is coming now." Grace indicated towards the stable where a tall, lean man was walking towards them. His broad shoulders, flannel shirt, jeans and well-worn boots along with his un-kempt hair didn't much resemble the picture on Redemption's web-site but, in fact, much more closely resemble Kelsie's former classmate. His sparkling blue eyes confirmed it: Brice Turner was briskly walking towards them.

"Hey Grace, is this our new guest?"

A disarming smile radiated confidence as Brice put his hand out to shake Jessie's, who was slow to extend his own. But he got caught up in Brice's enthusiasm and eventually gave him a firm handshake.

"Good to meet you. I'm Brice. Welcome to Redemption!" Brice then turned to Kelsie. "And you must be Jessie's mother. Brice Turner." He shook her hand with confidence and his expression showed not the least bit of recognition.

Kelsie was thrown off-guard by the vast differences between the man that stood before her and the boy she remembered from her youth. Gone was the long, ratty hair, dirty jeans and worn out boots. Instead, the man standing before her had a fine, lean figure, clearly showing he spent time keeping himself fit but not so much that he looked like he lived at the gym. His hair was shorter but not short, neater but not neat, with a light hint of premature grey showing at the temples. His eyes were still something to get lost in but age was showing on his face, likely the result of a hard-lived youth, which was what worried Kelsie the most. Considering his current position, she figured he must have grown out of the reckless ways of his younger years but she needed to know for sure.

"Hello, yes, I'm Kelsie." She was disappointed that her response stumbled from her lips as if from a nervous school-girl.

"Nice to meet you." Brice flashed that disarming smile again as they shook hands. Then he turned to his new charge.

"Jessie, I'm going to be your counselor while you're here so we'll get to know each other real well but for now, Grace is going to get you checked in, show you around and get you to your bunk while I chat with your mother for a few minutes." He gave Jessie a firm pat on the shoulder.

"C'mon Jessie, grab your stuff and let's get you situated," Grace chimed in brightly.

Jessie wondered if he was going to have to suffer the type exuberant attitude Brice and Grace displayed from everyone at Redemption as he took his bag from the back of the car. Feeling as if he was entering some sort of cult, he followed Grace.

"Hold on there," Kelsie called out. "I need a hug goodbye."

Jessie stopped and turned around as she walked over to him. He wanted to be embarrassed as any teen should be when his mother demanded a hug. But he strangely felt as though a hug from his mother was just what he wanted at that point. It was an odd feeling that he didn't understand. She wrapped him in her arms as she felt him do the same. She sadly realized it was the first real hug they had shared in 18 months.

"Please use this opportunity for what it is," she whispered in his ear. "A chance to get your life back!" She pulled back from him so she could look him squarely in the eyes. "I need you to come back to me. I love you more than anything."

Jessie looked at her with a hint of moisture gathering in his eyes. "Love you too Mom" was all he said as he turned to follow Grace, who was enthusiastically walking towards the main building. He caught up to her quickly, following a few steps behind. He made no attempt to hide the fact he was dreading what was ahead.

Brice silently let Kelsie watch her son walk away for a few moments before speaking. "I've studied his case file. Don't worry, he'll be fine."

She spoke as she continued to watch Jessie disappear from sight when he entered the main building. "I wish I shared your optimism." She turned towards Brice, feeling confrontational; protective. "You don't even know him yet so how can you know he will be alright?"

Brice smiled. "While it may not feel like it, you aren't the first parent I've seen in this situation. I know it's not easy coming from a well-to-do situation and dropping your child off in a place like this. But

I've seen this enough to know that even if it looks like the situation is beyond hope, it's not."

Kelsie was annoyed by his assumption of her situation. "And how exactly do you know anything about our 'well-to-do' situation?"

"Like I said," Brice smiled. "I've studied his file…thoroughly. Don't worry, he's in good hands."

"And are those hands going to be able to bring back the happy young man I used to know?" Kelsie was getting more and more annoyed by Brice's arrogance. Especially since she knew so many details of his past.

"Well, that really depends on him. He has to want our help. And if he does, he'll have all of it he can handle."

"What if he thinks he doesn't *need* your help?"

"He won't be the first. So we'll have to help him realize he does need it. And *want* it."

Kelsie wasn't sure if Brice was arrogant, self-confident or delusional. Or maybe he was as good as he clearly thought he was. But regardless, she was desperate for him to understand her situation. "If you've actually read his file as thoroughly as you claim, then you know he's all I have. So I need you to not give up on him. Ever. Even if he doesn't seem to care or be interested in what you are trying to do. It's imperative you understand that."

Brice looked Kelsie straight on. "You have my word. He'll get my full attention and all the help my experience and training can provide."

Experience, Kelsie said to herself. *You've got plenty of that.*

Brice continued to stare at Kelsie, unsure of what it was that seemed slightly familiar about her. "Kelsie is a beautiful name. Don't know that I've ever met someone with that name before."

You have got to be kidding me, Kelsie thought. *I'm bringing my troubled son to you and you're going to flirt with me?!*

"So, you don't remember me."

Brice gave her a genuinely puzzled expression. "I'm sorry, should I?"

"We were in the same class at Central High School, although I don't recall you actually being at school that much. And when you were there, you were usually too busy being a trouble-maker and teasing me and my friends to really accomplish anything. To be perfectly honest, I'm surprised you graduated."

Brice was caught off-guard and suddenly embarrassed at the reminder of his past from a mother who had just brought her son to his facility for help, a facility that could have helped him in his youth. He looked at the ground as he spoke. "I did, but just barely." Then he regained his composure and faced Kelsie squarely, staring straight into her eyes. "And, yes, I was a bit of a trouble-maker but I honestly don't recall anyone in my class who looked like you."

"That's because I didn't look like this in school. Picture braces on my teeth and short frizzy hair. Then you might remember me."

He continued to stare at her for several moments as he recalled his unpleasant youth. "Well, I can honestly say that it looks like both of us have grown a lot since then."

"Have you?" Kelsie wasn't going to let him charm his way out of a conversation that was clearly uncomfortable for him. "I was very surprised to see it's you running this facility. Doesn't really seem like a vocation that matches someone who spent most of his teenage years in trouble with the law while at the same time being so well-suited to making the lives of his classmates miserable."

Brice continued to be surprised by her. "Wow, it seems as though I remember school a whole lot differently than you do."

"Because I remember how it really was. I'm thinking you were too high back then to remember anything at all."

Kelsie clearly had a different impression of their time in school than Brice did but he realized she had a valid point. He had spent a good part of his youth using various substances to help him escape his own demons. But in the long run, they did nothing to help his situation and, in fact, had made it worse for him in many ways. He was thankful every day that he had left those self-destructive ways behind him along with the many things he did which had adversely affected others. He had made his peace with his misspent youth and over the years had managed to put those events away in a part of his memory that he rarely revisited. So he definitely was not prepared for this conversation at all. It was clear Kelsie was bent on bringing up memories best forgotten and he wasn't certain to what end she was doing it. But he was starting to warm up to the confrontation she was putting forth.

"Tell me something. If you have so many bad memories surrounding me in school, why did you bring your son here? You know as well as I do there are plenty of other programs you could have chosen. So what makes you think a miscreant like myself could possibly provide the help your son needs?"

It was a valid question to which Kelsie wasn't sure she had a good answer. "It's hard to say." She folded her arms and spoke honestly. "But I'm seriously starting to think I made a mistake."

Brice's expression was questioning but before he could offer his thoughts, she continued.

"However, you use animals as part of your therapy. Jessie loves animals. So I'm hoping that aspect of your program will help to bring about the change that he...we...so desperately need."

"Glad that detail caught your eye. It's one of the keys to our success." Finally, he was getting some satisfaction out of their conversation. "And speaking of success, I'm certain our success rate also caught your eye."

She wasn't sure if it was smugness, satisfaction or confidence he was exuding but she knew from what she had read that it appeared Brice's program had helped a lot of people. After all, it was the deciding factor in her decision. "Yes, clearly you have the highest success rate of all the programs within 100 miles. Any idea why that is?"

"Could it possibly be that we know what we are doing?"

"Clearly. But I'm curious as to *how* you know what you are doing."

"Our rate of success is a reflection of our pasts. All of the counselors here have been in similar positions that the people enrolled in our program now find themselves. Everyone here is a former "trouble-maker". We know first-hand what it's like to be in these kid's positions. Fortunately, we all came out the other side as better people because someone helped us to figure out why we were acting out. We don't lecture here. We don't preach. We understand what these kids are going through so we help them to figure things out so they can turn themselves around. You may not want to believe it, but the part of my life you so vividly remember is all in the past. I'm not the same person I was in school. But my past informs me of ways I can help these kids figure out how they can have a better future."

Kelsie looked towards the main building as she recalled the sight of her son entering it moments earlier, feeling as though it was an eternity ago. Then she turned to stare Brice in the eye as she spoke. "Then I'm going to expect you to use all of the experience I personally know you have to help my son not continue to be a troubled teen."

She stared at her speechless former nemesis for several moments before turning to walk back to her car. As she got in and prepared to drive away, Brice was beginning to remember her from school and found himself wishing he had had the good sense to get to know her back then. *She might have been able to set me straight* he thought.

***

The main building of Redemption was sprawling, built in the style of a log cabin in the hopes of helping the people who came there feel relaxed. The reception area was informal. No desk or counter area with computer screens and paperwork scattered everywhere was anywhere to be seen. A fireplace on one wall seemed to invite people to sit and converse while the vaulted wood ceiling gave the space a larger-than-it-was feel. Comfortable looking furniture was spread throughout the area allowing people to sit and relax in small groups or alone. A short corridor off the main area led to the mess hall, where Jessie spied ping-pong and pool tables along the back wall. It all seemed…inviting to Jessie as he and Grace emerged from it after completing the check-in process, which to Jessie's surprise consisted of simply writing his name on a clipboard hanging next to the front door.

"We keep things informal wherever we can around here," Grace explained. "Every day when you enter the main building for breakfast, sign in on this clipboard. Proves you were here. Any other formalities you need to know about will be taken care of when you meet with Brice during your first session together."

Grace was still enthusiastic but had a relaxed, light air about her that made Jessie feel more comfortable than he ever imagined he would be in the place where he now found himself. As she showed him around the main building, Jessie noted that everyone he saw had a relaxed demeanor. Grace introduced him to a few of the people they passed but Jessie knew he would never remember any of their names. That didn't bother him though. He wasn't there to make friends. He actually wasn't sure what he was there to do…other than trying to stay out of jail.

When the two exited the main facility, Grace pointed out the bunk houses behind the building along with the stable and corral where Jessie saw several people with horses. A few dogs and cats were running around as well but it was the horses that held his attention. The majestic sight of someone riding such a large and powerful animal had always fascinated Jessie. He had actually never seen a horse up close. He hoped he'd have a chance to do more than that while he was there.

As he continued to survey the area further, he noticed his mother proceeding down the long driveway, starting her journey home. Suddenly, Jessie felt completely alone. And he hated the feeling.

Chapter Five

Jessie awoke after a night that was anything but restful. He had slept sporadically and during the hours he lay awake, he thought about his situation. While it was well documented in his court records *when* his troubles started, he wasn't sure *why* he started acting out in a way that got him into trouble. At first, he was mad and bored so shoplifting little things gave him a jolt of…he wasn't sure what. What he was sure of was the fact that his best friend quickly distanced himself the first time Jessie got caught. He didn't care. He didn't feel like hanging out with him or anyone anymore. But the more he was on his own, the more his mind came up with ridiculous things to do for thrills, things that he knew were wrong. He wasn't certain why he didn't care about the fact that he was suddenly doing things he never would have done before. The thought of disappointing his parents was something he had never wanted to face. For Jessie, his father telling him that he was disappointed in his son was worse than any punishment either of his parents could have imposed when he was younger. But somehow that just didn't seem to matter anymore.

Finally, as the sun began to rise, a bell sounded that alerted everyone in the building it was time to start the day. He had expected the bunk house to be like a military barracks with rows of beds filled with troubled teenagers from end-to-end. However, he was thankful to find he had a room which he shared with only one other person. Actually, it was a space containing two beds, two desks, two chairs and a rod on which he could hang some clothes. It certainly wasn't big on amenities but the bed was surprisingly comfortable and the blanket was warm and soft. All things considered, so far, he thought it might be possible that the time he would spend at Redemption might be tolerable.

The walls that made up the "rooms" were only seven feet tall and the ceilings were ten feet but Jessie appreciated that even walls which fell short of the ceiling did provide a bit of privacy. However, they didn't prevent him from hearing his fellow "inmates" snoring through the night. Some were impressively loud. But that wasn't what had kept him awake. He knew that the impending day would include the first in a series of sessions where he would be expected to talk, to explain himself, to express his feelings, and eventually…. to change. And he had no idea how he was going to do any of it.

He rose from his bed and proceeded to make it, mostly to kill time. Considering the room's sparse furnishings and the fact that his roommate seemed to be an early riser as he was nowhere to be seen, there wasn't much keeping Jessie there so he dressed and headed towards the mess hall prior to the breakfast bell sounding.

Jessie made little eye-contact with the other kids as he weaved his way through the food line. It all looked edible but nothing like the breakfast his mother would make him every Saturday. But it wasn't Saturday and he wasn't home. *This is gonna be a long 30 days* he thought to himself as he found a seat and settled in to eat.

"Good morning Jessie. Hope your first night was restful." Grace seemed to appear out of nowhere and was suddenly sitting across from him. Jessie wasn't prepared for her perkiness so early in the day. "Just wanted to remind you about your 9:00 meeting with Brice."

"Morning Grace." He didn't want to be rude but he wasn't interested in early morning conversation. "I'll be there."

"Great. Are you getting along OK so far?" She seemed genuinely concerned about him but her enthusiasm made Jessie a bit uncomfortable.

"Good so far," he replied, hoping she would leave him to eat in peace. He wasn't planning on making friends while he was there and he definitely wasn't planning on getting to know the people who worked there.

"Glad to hear it. I'll see you later." And with that, Grace disappeared as fast as she had appeared.

***

Brice waited patiently for Jessie's first appointment with him, hoping he would show up, whether he was on time or not. The first session with each new participant in the program was always the hardest and sometimes never happened. The policy of having no locks keeping people at Redemption meant that from time to time, kids would leave. Most eventually came back but if they didn't, it only made things worse for them with the courts or their parents, depending on how they came to be there. If participation had been court mandated and the participant left before they completed the program, they most certainly wouldn't find the next place they were assigned to easier to deal with.

Brice's office was purposely warm and inviting, with a lived-in look that included pictures scattered throughout of him skiing, hiking, horseback-riding and paddle boarding. What did not appear on his walls, desks or shelves were family pictures of any sort. His diploma and licenses were framed and discreetly displayed in a corner where they were behind the door when it was open, which was basically anytime Brice was not meeting with a program participant. By law, he had to display them but he felt it was unnecessary to remind people of his training in case it made them feel self-conscious. While program participants needed help, he didn't feel it was necessary to remind them they were seeing a therapist every time they walked into his office. He wanted them to be relaxed and didn't want his office to make them feel as though they were under a spotlight. A large window allowed a clear view of the stables and the forest beyond while flooding the room with light. He always kept the shades up as he thought the view helped to complete the relaxing atmosphere he was striving to provide.

The furnishings were also chosen to make people feel comfortable, with soft, deep chairs instead of stiff, uncomfortable office furniture. Small tables sat next to each chair in the room, each holding a box of tissues. He kept a small refrigerator stocked with bottled water for instances when sessions involved so much talking…or crying…that fluid replenishment was needed. And a bear-skin rug under the table that sat between the two chairs facing each other served as a good conversation starter, if needed. No couches were in any of the offices at Redemption. Since it wasn't a typical facility where psychiatrists met patient after patient, Brice never wanted the facility to feel as if it was. He kept his desk clear of insignificant clutter so as not to appear disorganized but it contained just enough paperwork to confirm his days were busy.

Being in charge of a facility that was usually at capacity, the administrative duties Brice had to complete kept him occupied to the point that he wasn't able to meet with as many participants as he did during his first years there. But he always kept his hand in the core goal of the facility, which was to help as many kids as possible. So he had a select few program participants he would work with as their main counselor. Jessie's case had caught his eye when he did his daily review of incoming kids a few days prior and he felt as though he could be very effective in helping the new participant. But after meeting his mother, he was wondering if he should let Jessie work with another counselor. He didn't want her tainted memories of their time in school to possibly hinder Jessie's success.

Brice was relieved when he sensed a figure had appeared in his doorway. He looked up from his paperwork as Jessie entered the room. He wasn't surprised when Jessie didn't say anything but simply flopped into one of the soft chairs in the middle of the room. Clearly he wanted to be anywhere but where he was, which was understandable and not at all uncommon for newcomers. Still, the process needed to start and Brice was thankful Jessie showed up. He took it as a good sign, even though he knew that, if asked, Jessie would never admit he was there for any other reason than it was mandated.

Brice let the silence in the room stand for several moments. He remained seated at his desk as Jessie sat still, not moving at all, staring at the floor.

"Good morning Jessie. Hope you slept well."

Brice watched as Jessie didn't respond in any way to his unoriginal conversation starter. He eventually continued.

"So you know by now that I'm going to be helping you over the next 30 days. We'll be meeting on a regular basis and while we are together, you can talk to me about whatever you want. We can discuss what's going on with you now, what's happened in the past, things that concern you about the future and anything that's going through your head that you may not understand. Whatever you want. Nothing is off-limits"

Jessie spoke without looking up. "So, you're my shrink. I get it."

"That's not the word I would use."

"Is there a word that's more accurate?" Jessie pressed. "Aren't I here so you can get into my head and figure out why I'm screwed up? Aren't you supposed to straighten me and the other inmates out?"

Brice winced. He never wanted to hear terms like "inmate", "shrink", "therapy" or anything that made the program participants feel like they were criminals or crazy used by anyone. To Brice, words with negative connotations could make someone like Jessie feel like less of a person, which was counterintuitive to what Redemption was all about.

"For the record, you aren't "screwed-up". You've made mistakes that have gotten you into trouble. So we're here to figure out, together, why you did those things. Our regular meetings are meant as a time for us to just talk, about whatever you want to discuss. There's no judgment in here."

Jessie finally looked at Brice. "Oh, so you're my friend, is that it?" Jessie's voice took on a snarky tone that wasn't surprising to Brice.

"Hopefully, one day. But for now I just want to be someone you feel comfortable with so we can discuss what's going on."

Jessie peered out the window, fixated on the activity surrounding the stables.

"My main goal is to help you stay out of jail or juvenile detention or any other type of restrictive situation," Brice continued. "But I also want to help you figure out anything that's causing you confusion, which may be contributing to your current situation."

Brice got up from his chair and came around his desk to sit opposite Jessie, hoping a less formal seating arrangement might help their conversation progress. "I want our time together to be helpful to you. Everything we talk about is confidential so nothing will make it beyond these walls. You can feel free to talk to me about anything." He paused, smiled, then continued. "And trust me, it'll be very hard for you to surprise me."

He wasn't certain but he thought he saw a reaction from Jessie. Perhaps a slight smile. Or maybe he sensed a look of "don't be so sure". Still, he didn't seem to be getting through to the center's newest resident. He decided to continue with some bland conversation. "So, are you settling in OK?"

Jessie shrugged without saying a word.

"I know you've met a few of the other kids and, of course, your roommate, so I hope you're getting comfortable. Just try not to think of your time here as punishment. That hasn't been determined yet so your time here will actually help to determine what your punishment will...or won't...be."

As Brice spoke, he could see that Jessie's interest was held by the activity he was viewing through the office window. The horses were being tended to by program participants under cloudy skies that would be threatening snow if the temperature was just a bit colder. But even under the persistent cloud cover, clearly what was going on outside was more enticing than the lop-sided conversation taking place inside his office. He knew it was time to change tactics.

"Clearly you aren't ready to talk. So just remember that, while we will have our regular meetings, I'm here whenever you need me. To talk...to listen...to practice singing Christmas carols...whatever."

Jessie looked at Brice as if he were crazy.

"So, you are listening!" He smiled his most reassuring smile as he looked Jessie in the eye.

Jessie gave Brice a hesitant smile, then returned his attention to the activity outside.

Brice was determined to keep things light for the moment. "OK, just so I know that I've hammered it into your head properly, give me an indication you understand you can come to me at any time."

Jessie nodded, looking slightly relieved that he had someone to talk to if he needed, which he did. Just not at that moment.

"Excellent! We're making progress already! So for now, go grab your coat and meet me at the front door. I want to introduce you to someone. And you won't even need to talk to him if you don't want." With no further explanation, Brice got up, grabbed the coat hanging on the back of his chair and put it on as he left his office.

Jessie quickly went to his room to retrieve his coat, hoping whatever Brice had planned meant he would be able to avoid a conversation he didn't want to have at that moment. He knew he was there to get himself straightened out so he could avoid a much more drastic situation but at that moment, his head was too jumbled up to talk. He simply didn't know how to express what he was feeling or thinking because he wasn't sure of it himself.

***

Brice and Jessie walked towards the stables without talking. As they got closer to the large red building, Jessie started to relax, allowing himself to feel excited at the possibility of spending time with some of the animals he saw all around him. In his mind, at that moment, anything was better than sitting in an office talking.

As they entered the stables, Jessie followed Brice, wondering what was in store. Most of the stalls were empty since so many horses were currently outside being tended to and ridden. As they passed by one of the few stalls with a horse inside, an attractive 19-year-old girl with shoulder-length brunette hair and trim, athletic figure emerged. She reminded him of a girl from his history class in whom he was interested, a feeling she hadn't shared.

Jessie instinctively smiled at her

Brice waved. "Morning April."

"Morning!"

Brice stopped to make proper introductions. April was immediately struck by Jessie's looks. Not gorgeous in the sense of a model, he was clearly hot in a way she appreciated immensely. His longish hair was tousled enough that it wasn't neat but it wasn't the typical mess that too many teens called a "style". Its dirty blonde color coupled with his deep blue eyes made his looks even more enticing. And it helped that he clearly didn't sit around playing video games all day as his physique was that of someone who was active, although the activities could easily have been of nefarious origin, considering where he was at the moment. Still, she appreciated the fact that he wore jeans that fit his toned butt instead of sagging like the ones worn by most boys Jessie's age. She didn't like that look and generally didn't like the boys who sported it either. But considering Jessie was at Redemption, April knew that she should curb any attraction she may feel for him since it probably wasn't appropriate. Still, she relished in the thought that Jessie was the type of young man that would annoy her father to no end if she were to bring him home to "meet the family". Her father was annoyed by seemingly anything she did.

As Jessie seemed fixated on her hazel eyes, April teased. "I saw you arrive yesterday. Glad to see you survived your first night."

A scowl covered Brice's face. "April, please don't make it sound like we do human sacrifices here," he chastised her. "You know we stopped doing that stuff last year!"

As April giggled, Brice was glad to see a genuine smile appear on Jessie's face.

Brice motioned Jessie over to the next stall where a beautiful chocolate-brown horse stood. "Jessie, I want to introduce you to Bailey. Like you, he's just arrived at Redemption. He's a rescue animal that came to us last week."

Jessie was puzzled. "A rescue animal?"

"That's right," Brice explained. "You see, we don't just rescue humans here. Animals need rescued just as much as people do. Animals that are being abused or neglected throughout the state are brought here so we can protect them and help them get over their trauma so they can be content around humans and, at the same time, they can help people like you."

"How's a horse gonna help me?"

"Because you'll be taking care of him while you're here."

Suddenly, Jessie's elation at being around animals was replaced with a degree of panic. He didn't know anything about caring for a horse and wasn't certain if his counselor was joking or serious.

Brice could see the trepidation in Jessie's expression. "Don't worry," he reassured. "You'll both learn a path forward together. So far, Bailey hasn't connected with anyone here. He won't let anyone saddle or ride him, most likely because he was rescued from a horse farm where he was abused. Bailey here doesn't trust anyone so right off the bat the two of you have something in common. Animals have great intuition so I think that you two will be able to help each other."

Jessie stood and looked at Bailey for several moments. The noble beast stood with his head up, as if he knew he was the subject of conversation. His ears were perked up and his tail was constantly swishing at the backside of his sleek brown body. But his eyes seemed sad to Jessie, although he had no idea how he would know what the eyes of a happy horse would look like by comparison. It was just a sense he had…felt.

Jessie finally spoke as his concern grew. "But I really don't know anything about caring for a horse. I don't want to mess things up."

"You mean for someone other than yourself?"

Jessie discomfort was palpable. He knew caring for an animal was a big responsibility, one that he never had to learn. He was starting to feel like he was being set up for failure by the very person who was supposed to be helping him.

"Don't worry," Brice continued. "It's not that tough. But it's important that certain things be done regularly because Bailey's welfare depends on you. So you may need to ask someone for help to figure things out. Don't be afraid to do that."

Before Jessie could say anything, Brice turned and left the stable, winking at April as he caught her eye.

Jessie stood in the stall, staring at Bailey, who had moved to one end of the stall, seemingly nervous. Jessie wondered how he would even know if a horse was nervous since he knew nothing about them. He stood still for several moments as he tried to calm the heart pounding in his chest. Eventually, he instinctively approached Bailey slowly, bringing his hands up to the long, strong neck and gently stroking it from behind Bailey's ear down to his broad shoulders. He continued repeating the action without making a sound.

April peaked into the stall. "You doing OK?"

"I'm not sure," Jessie replied nervously.

"It looks like you're doing fine at the moment."

"But I wasn't joking when I told Brice I don't know anything about horses."

"Don't worry, they aren't complicated. So far your natural instincts seem to be right," April encouraged. "He seems to like what you're doing or he wouldn't let you continue."

Jessie was certain she was putting him on but he didn't stop the gentle stroking of Bailey's neck. The horse did seem to enjoy it and Jessie had no idea what else he could do at that moment.

"Just remember that, like Brice said, it's important that certain things are done daily and regularly." April spoke calmly but with a gentle firmness that told Jessie she knew what she was talking about. "His well-being depends completely on you taking care of his needs. Treat him right and he'll do the same for you." She paused as she still sensed a bit of panic in Jessie. "I'll be glad to help you, if you'd like."

Jessie breathed a sigh of relief. "I think for Bailey's sake, that's a good idea."

"No problem." April motioned for Jessie to follow her into the next stall. "Watch what I'm doing with Beau." April ran her hand along the horse's strong, smooth back. "I got here just before you and I was talking to Beau before I started his daily routine."

"You talk to your horse?" Jessie was certain she was trying to make him look foolish.

"Absolutely! Horses, and animals in general, are great listeners! Beau and I are best-buds, right Beau?" She patted the neck of the jet-black horse as he nuzzled into her face. "Animals understand a lot more than you think. Beau may not know all the words I say but he understands the tone of my voice. An animal can sense when you're happy, sad, nervous, tense, angry, whatever…just from your tone and your mannerisms. Since I'm going to be working in his space, I want to make sure he doesn't feel threatened by me in any way. A nice calm chat before I start the daily routine, along with a handful of oats, goes a long way towards letting him know that he's safe with me and helps to keep him calm." April nodded towards Bailey's stall. "You already figured out the right way to keep Bailey calm."

"I did?" Jessie wasn't aware that he had been doing anything right, whether it pertained to Bailey or his life.

"You were patting and scratching his neck, nice and calmly."

"Yeah, but I wasn't trying to do anything. It just seemed like it made sense."

"So it seems you have a good instinct about horses." April displayed a genuine smile that, along with her encouraging words, suddenly provided Jessie a slight feeling of elation.

Oddly enough, it was a similar feeling he had experienced when he was doing things he knew he shouldn't.

April motioned to the next stall. "Why don't you spend a few more minutes with Bailey before we get started."

Jessie turned to return to Bailey's stall.

"Don't forget the oats!" April reminded him.

He stuck his hand in the bag hanging on the wood beam between the stalls and approached Bailey slowly, lightly patting and scratching his neck, the horse's shiny coat feeling pleasantly soft on his hand. He brought the oats to Bailey's mouth and smiled as the horse eagerly ate. After several moments, Jessie whispered into Bailey's ear.

"I hope you don't get tired of listening to my problems."

Chapter Six

Tina approached the coffee shop door precisely at 7:00 am Tuesday morning after the long Thanksgiving weekend. As a real estate broker, her work day could start at any time but being an early riser meant that her day started earlier than most brokers, which often worked to her advantage. This morning though, she wanted to know how it went when Kelsie dropped Jessie off at Redemption the previous day. Knowing she wouldn't want to relive the event too soon after it took place, rather than calling her friend the previous evening, Tina gave her some time but insisted on meeting in person to see for herself how Kelsie was holding up

The routine the two enjoyed ever since Kelsie had moved back to town was to meet at their favorite coffee shop every morning for the crucial morning jump-start that got their brains ready for the day ahead. Some days they met only briefly if one or both of them had a busy day planned. Then some days they would sit for a while and relax before their respective days started, talking about anything and everything. Tina knew Kelsie would be in a hurry since she had taken the previous day off and needed to get caught up at work. But she was keen on making sure her bestie was doing alright and would therefore insist they relax for at least a few minutes and talk about how everything had gone.

As Tina came through the door, a handsome man about her age was coming out, seemingly in a hurry. But he gave a long pause to allow himself time to appreciate the beauty that was before him. Tina's flawless brown skin, athletic build and striking features often attracted gazes that she didn't pay much attention to. But on this morning, she was very appreciative of the attention being shown her by this particular individual. His broad shoulders and attention to grooming were very attractive but his piercing green eyes were what held her attention the most. She knew for certain she would have re-membered him if she had ever seen him in the shop previously.

"Excuse me," he said as he paused. He was clearly flustered but she wasn't sure if it was because he was late or because he almost plowed into her. "I need to do a better job of watching where I'm going!" His genuine smile revealed the brightest white teeth she had ever seen while his sharp style of dress was as eye-catching as his radiant smile and eyes. And his smooth voice confirmed to her that he was some-one she wanted to know better.

"No worries," she responded instinctively. "I could stand to slow down a bit myself." She smiled the best smile she could conjure up, trying not to look too eager to speak further. Yet that's exactly what she wanted!

He seemed to fumble with exactly what he should do next but simply stepped aside, allowing Tina to enter. He watched her as she moved through the doorway, her enticing figure passing by him smoothly.

"I hope you have a nice day." He smiled as he stared at her for a long moment. Then he turned to leave.

She knew she had to say something. But her usually witty nature failed her. "You too," she called after him. *You too?!?* she chastised her-self. *That's all you could come up with? The first good looking, new man you've had seen in forever just passed by and you come up with the lamest line in the book!?!*

And so their brief time together came to an end as quickly as it started. After exchanging nothing further than a smile between them, he was through the door and out onto the busy sidewalk.

Tina was still giving herself a hard time as she spotted Kelsie at their usual table.

As her friend approached, Kelsie couldn't help but tease. "I was about to dig my phone out and call the fire department. Sparks were flying!"

Tina sat down hard, exasperated with herself. "Don't I know it! And I could barely get two words out of my mouth! I'm truly hopeless."

"Considering how confident you usually are, I'm surprised you don't already know his sign, what he does for a living and have a date scheduled for Friday night!"

Tina smiled and quickly held up a finger. "The first flaw in your plan is that you know Friday night is our night. I'm not going to give up us sharing a nice bottle of wine and spending time unwinding for some random guy!"

Kelsie gave her friend a look that said, *you expect me to believe that?* Which made them both burst with laughter.

"But today, I was seemingly back in high school, afraid to talk to any boy." Tina was not at all happy with herself. "But I'll make sure I have something clever to say if I ever see him in here again. I'm hoping he's new in town and this place becomes part of his usual routine."

Kelsie knew Tina had been alone for way too long and she wanted to help her out of her drought. "Don't bother coming up with something clever to say. Just introduce yourself and let the conversation happen naturally." Her friend was always able to come up with clever things to say when she had a few moments to think about them. But Kelsie knew that sometimes just being natural was the better move. She motioned towards the coffee shop counter. "And before you leave today, ask Joan if she's ever seen him in here. You know she remembers everyone and what they drink."

"Good idea. And if she doesn't know, I just may camp out here for a week or two to see if he shows up again!" Tina was already hopeful as she lifted the lid on her coffee to blow on the steamy brew Kelsie had obtained for her. "So, how did it go yesterday? I hoped you might call me when you got back."

"I'm sorry I didn't but after I left there, I took my time driving back, taking the opportunity to really think about everything."

It wasn't difficult to see the worry in Kelsie's expression. And why wouldn't it be there? "I hope you aren't blaming yourself for this situation."

"Why shouldn't I blame myself?" Kelsie looked up with moist eyes. "Jessie's been headed down the wrong road ever since we've been on our own. I'm the one who's responsible for keeping him safe and moving in the right direction but clearly I'm doing it all wrong." Frustration was building within her and as she spoke, she could feel herself getting more and more anxious because of her perceived failure.

Tina placed her hand on Kelsie's. "Honey, you can't blame yourself! You were thrown into a horrible situation and you had to figure out not only how to keep Jessie grounded but how to keep yourself sane. These aren't tasks that anyone could do easily. Just because Jessie has taken a wrong turn doesn't mean you did anything wrong. In fact, you've done a lot right. You both have a roof over your heads, food on the table and a whole lot more. Jessie just needs help figuring a few things out and it's not a failure on your part that you couldn't help him do it. So it's OK that you are seeking professional help for him." She hoped her words were not falling on ears that couldn't hear her over the noise she knew was buzzing inside Kelsie's head.

She knew Tina's words made sense but the over-achieving mother in Kelsie couldn't let herself off-the-hook. "Well, it's pretty much out of my hands now. He's at Redemption and I can only hope and pray they can help him."

Tina hesitated in asking but couldn't help herself. "Did you run into *him* while you were there?"

"Oh yes." Kelsie's expression changed from desperation to determination. "Turns out he's going to be Jessie's counselor."

The looked of apprehensive fear on Tina's face spoke volumes.

"And I made it clear that I expected him to do whatever it takes to help my son."

Tina shook her head. "I can't believe someone who should have been a participant in that type of program is actually in charge of a facility like that. Please tell me he's changed."

She gave a slight shrug. "I don't know. I mean, I was hesitant to take Jessie there because of him," Kelsie said as she stared at her coffee cup. "But I have to admit, he seemed much different than when we were in school." She raised her eyes to meet Tina's. "He'd have to be, right?" She wasn't sure if she was trying to convince her friend or herself.

Tina was skeptical. "How was he different?"

"He seemed...grounded, actually genuine. Nothing like the person we remember. I wouldn't have known it was him if I didn't *know* it was him. I really was surprised. And relieved."

The two sat silently for several moments.

Kelsie threw up her hands as she finally spoke. "But, of course, all I did was remind him of what a loser he was in school."

"Nothing wrong with that, as far as I'm concerned. It's good for him to realize that you know him better than most parents who bring their kids to him for help."

"I don't disagree. But he really seems different. He has a rugged charm about him now that no doubt helps him win over the kids entrusted to him. But he's also very nice and easy going, even while all I did was remind him of his misspent youth and what a troublemaker he was back then. Definitely not my finest moment."

Tina sat back in her chair, aghast. "Oh no," she muttered.

"What's wrong?"

"I don't believe it." She stared at Kelsie across the table.

"What is wrong with you?" Kelsie was getting concerned. "You look like you've seen a ghost."

Tina shook her head. "Not a ghost. Just a person from the past." She sat forward and leaned across the table. "You always had a bit of a thing for him. I could see it sometimes in the way you looked at him back then. And now I see that same look in your eyes."

"Oh, don't be silly." Kelsie blushed as she paused for a moment. "Everyone fantasizes about the bad-boy in school every once in a while, don't they?"

Tina's expression showed she wasn't buying anything her friend was dishing out.

"Whatever." Kelsie gave her a dismissive wave of her hand. "Even if I was thinking along those lines, which I am definitely not, I did everything within my power to squash any possibility of anything happening after only being around him for a few minutes."

Tina stood and grabbed her coat. "I doubt you squashed anything so much that it couldn't be revived with a phone call." She winked at a doe-eyed Kelsie as she put on her coat. "I've got to get to the office but call me later. I'm certain we aren't done talking about this."

"There is no *this*," Kelsie insisted, once again not certain of who she was trying to convince. But she had to get to her office as well so anything Tina might think was happening would have to wait as she too put on her coat and started for the door.

***

Kelsie walked into her office in a foul mood. And her coworkers could sense it. During the walk between the coffee shop and her office, her mood had darkened. The thought of Jessie being so far away and her not being able to talk to him or see for herself how he was doing had affected her mood in the most negative way possible.

Few people at her office knew the details of Jessie's situation or why she had taken off the previous day. She felt confident in her abilities to separate work from home so that very few people she spent time with every day knew what was going on. But her assistant was well aware of what was happening in Kelsie's life and she was certain he kept her secrets to himself. She thought herself fortunate to have someone she could trust close by every day. It helped on those occasions when she had to abruptly leave or came in late because of a situation that had arisen regarding Jessie.

She also felt fortunate that her boss was understanding and didn't necessarily want to know the details. All he really cared about was if she got her work done. Kelsie truly felt blessed that she had stumbled into her current position when her family moved back to her hometown well outside of Boston. She could do the job in her sleep so when there was upheaval in her home situation, which there had been far too much of in the previous two years, knowing her work situation was stable provided her a foundation to lean on.

Jasper entered her office hesitantly. "You OK?"

Kelsie appreciated his simple question. She knew he wouldn't pry for details but would also listen if she wanted to use him as a sounding board. "I'm fine, thanks." She looked at him and could see he didn't believe her but he went ahead and started updating her on the morning's business.

"OK then. Don't forget you have an 11:30 lunch meeting with Jenn to discuss your joint project. She needs updated numbers, which I have already sent to you for review and approval. And then there is a conference call at 2:00 with a potential new client. I've sent you the background information already." Jasper paused and looked at his boss. "And you aren't hearing a word I'm saying." He flashed an understanding smile that she had seen all too often lately.

"I'm so sorry. I actually am listening but my mind is elsewhere."

"Understandable. You want me to come back?"

"No, thanks. I know you've already given me all the information I need, like you always do, so I'll go through it all and let you know if I have any questions." She smiled as she looked at him with an appreciative stare. "Thanks Jasper."

"Of course. And if you need anything, just let me know." He turned to leave.

"Can you give me a new brain? Mine is all mixed up."

He turned to her and winked. "I have a feeling there's a story there."

"There is." Kelsie hesitated but decided to let him know the latest development in the 'Jessie saga'. After she told him the general details, she paused before continuing. "Let's just say I'm not at my best right now."

"I don't think anyone would fault you for that. Jessie's situation is tough."

She didn't go into too many details about Brice, feeling Jasper might easily think she was crazy for leaving her son with someone like him.

"Just have some faith. Hopefully this place will help Jessie in a way that makes things easier for both of you."

Kelsie looked up. "From your lips to God's ears." She smiled weakly.

Jasper gave her another wink and turned to leave. "Just let me know if you need anything. And try not to worry. It won't change anything."

Alone in her office, Kelsie sat at her desk and sighed heavily, trying to relax. She looked at the folders on her desk, then opened her e-mails and found 27 new ones she would need to respond to that morning. Her office was comfortable, with plants in the corners and a few plaques on the wall, semi hidden behind the door. She felt it was ostentatious when she walked into someone's office and the walls were plastered with commendations and degrees. But she had to display a few so she did it in a way that didn't slap visitors in the face. She didn't need all that to show she was good at her job. Her position in the company and the results she generated spoke volumes.

As she looked at the familiar surroundings, she kept staring at her phone. Perhaps Tina was right. A phone call might put her mind at ease. Brice seemed different…better…and she felt bad for bringing up the past so fervently during their brief reunion. She kept staring at her phone until she picked it up and punched in a number.

The phone on Brice's desk rang – the line that was only used by parents wanting an update on their kids. He usually dreaded answering it since often he couldn't share the information parents were seeking. It wasn't that he didn't want to share good news – or bad news. Sometimes parents needed to hear what they didn't want to hear. But regardless, often there were circumstances where he either was bound by a court order to keep the program participant's progress confidential and sometimes he just didn't want to argue with a parent who didn't like or agree with his assessment of their child. But today, he decided he wouldn't make the parent who was calling leave a message.

"Hello."

"Hi Brice. It's Kelsie, from yesterday." She was suddenly nervous.

"Oh, hello."

To Kelsie, his response was cool, unemotional and hard-to-read. "You don't sound very surprised to hear from me."

He chuckled. "You aren't the first anxious mother to call me the day after dropping their child off here. I'm actually surprised it took you this long to check on him."

"I'll admit it wasn't easy to keep myself from calling before now."

"It's understandable. But don't worry, Jessie's doing fine. I just introduced him to the horse he'll be tending to while he's here."

"He's caring for a horse?" Kelsie's surprise was evident in her voice. "Isn't that a lot of responsibility for him with everything he's going through? He doesn't even know anything about horses!"

"Don't worry mother," Brice stated sarcastically. "By the end of today, he'll know everything he needs to about caring for his horse." He wasn't at all surprised by her response. "And I have a strong feeling that some responsibility is exactly what he needs right now."

Kelsie didn't appreciate the implication. "Are you saying I coddle my son?"

There was a significant pause in the conversation as Brice contemplated his next words carefully. Ultimately, he simply spoke his mind. "Do you always take immediate offense to anything someone says…or just what I say?"

Suddenly, Kelsie felt very foolish. She hadn't wanted her call to be confrontational. In fact, she had planned for it to be the opposite. But thanks again to her tainted memories of the person she was speaking to, the conversation had gone exactly in the direction she was trying to avoid. "Sorry. I'm certain you have my son's best interests in mind. I'm just nervous about this whole situation."

"Don't be." His tone started to soften. "I won't give him more that he can handle, even though you and he might not feel that way sometimes. But I promise he'll be fine while he's here."

"I'm going to hold you to that promise!"

"I'm not worried."

His voice showed no trace of concern. Kelsie wasn't sure why but she was feeling more confident in Jessie's chances for success the more she talked with Brice.

"If there isn't anything else, I have some things I need to take care of this morning." He wasn't in the mood for more confrontational conversation.

Kelsie hesitated, took a deep breath, and revealed the main reason for her call. "Sorry, I know you're busy but before I let you go, I want to apologize for my attitude yesterday. I feel I was a bit hard on you, letting memories of the past cloud my current perception of you." She struggled to banish the nervousness she was feeling from her voice as she continued. "I wanted you to know that I'm very sorry about that. It really was uncalled for."

Brice was, frankly, shocked. He never expected to hear those words emanate from her lips. "Well, I appreciate the apology but, truth be told, it's not necessary. I was anything but a model citizen when we were in school."

"True. But clearly you have changed or you wouldn't be where you are."

"Thanks for noticing," he replied, truly appreciating her words. "I've grown up from the person you knew in school."

"I believe you have and I'm sorry I didn't allow myself to see that yesterday. But believe me when I say I'm thankful for it. And I'm praying you can help my son to do the same."

"I'll do my best. After all, who better to help a troubled teen figure things out than a former troubled teen?" He wasn't sure she would appreciate his attempt to lighten the mood a bit.

All Kelsie could think to say was, "Thank you."

"Don't thank me yet. I haven't really done anything." He needed to temper her expectations, just in case. While he was confident in his ability to help Jessie, after their first session together his newest charge was clearly resisting. So there was always a chance he might not graduate from the program, regardless of how much effort was put forth on his behalf.

Brice was totally caught off-guard by the conversation he was having with Kelsie. Considering their encounter the previous day, he never dreamed he'd hear her admit that he had changed. Maybe she wasn't the stuck-up good girl he finally remembered when he looked through his eleventh grade school yearbook. And maybe she could help promote a change in Jessie, even though he was certain she had no clue how to do it.

"Tell you what. Why don't you come to the ranch this weekend?" Even though Redemption wasn't technically a ranch, Brice liked to refer to it as such rather than calling it the "center" or "facility".

The suggestion surprised her. "Do you think that's a good idea? I thought the plan was to separate Jessie from his life so he could get a better perspective on things."

"That's our usual M.O. But in some cases, like Jessie's, it makes sense to keep him in touch with his reality. I think it would do you both good to see each other on the weekends. Since you've probably told him that we knew each other years ago, he might learn some things about how people can change, for the better. I'm pretty sure we've both done that and your perspective will help him to see that change can be achieved."

Brice's statement surprised Kelsie. Had she really changed from her youth? She didn't feel as though she had. She never thought she needed to change so she had never contemplated whether or not she had. However, Brice's comment sparked a thought deep inside her that she realized she would have to consider. But for now, she needed to figure out how she should respond to the invitation.

"Do you really think seeing me will help?"

"I actually think it will help both of you. And hopefully you'll see Jessie making progress each week."

Suddenly, apprehension swelled up in Kelsie. "And what if I don't?"

"Then you don't," Brice stated matter-of-factly. "But it's what I see that matters to the judge. I'm thinking your visits could spark something in Jessie that will inform him of what he has to lose. Hopefully that will inspire him to want to make a change in his life."

Leaving her son the previous day had been one of the hardest things Kelsie had ever done so the thought of seeing Jessie on weekends without being able to take him home, along with the possibility of her not seeing much change in him was overwhelming to her. She didn't know if she could handle it. As she considered what she thought would be the best course of action, the pause in the conversation gave Brice the opportunity he wanted.

"So I'll see you Saturday," he quickly stated before ending the call.

Kelsie was stunned. And thankful she was sitting. *What actually just happened?* she asked herself. She tossed her thoughts around for several moments but finally realized that, if the head counselor at the camp where Jessie was supposed to get the help he needed had determined her visits could be of help to her son, she would absolutely be there. Besides, she wanted to know more about her son's counselor.

As Brice put down the phone, he wondered why he had suggested that Kelsie visit the ranch. It was true that sometimes it made sense for family members and others from a program participant's circle to visit them while they were at the facility. And he genuinely felt there was a chance it might help in Jessie's case. But he also wondered if he had invited Kelsie to visit for more selfish reasons. As he had strolled down memory lane after she left the previous day, he was reminded of so much. Beyond his mis-spent youth and the pain he likely caused others, including his best friend and people like Kelsie, he remembered that he had taken her for a spoiled brat back then, certain she would remain so throughout her entire life. He was starting to believe that was an unfortunate misconception on his part.

Chapter Seven

The morning after she spoke to Brice, Kelsie detailed their conversation to Tina during their regular morning coffee meeting. While the focus was on the fact that she was going to see Jessie on Saturday, Tina saw through Kelsie's genuine excitement regarding a visit with her son to what really had her fired up.

"Don't think I don't know what's going on here," Tina said with fierce determination that Kelsie knew all too well meant there was no sense in denying anything.

"First of all, you know me too damn well," Kelsie rolled her eyes as she spoke. "But what's the harm in finding out if Brice really has changed? You said yourself that he wouldn't be in his current position if he hadn't become a better person. So since that person is assigned to helping my son, I think it makes sense for me to make sure he's changed for the better."

"Correction, I think it was *you* who said that he must have changed his ways and at the time, I was certain you were trying to convince yourself that it was true for Jessie's sake." Tina squinted at Kelsie. "But now I'm pretty certain there is an additional reason why you want it to be true."

Tina wasn't wrong. Kelsie's life had been turned upside down with everything that had happened since she returned to her hometown. And her entire life centered around Jessie, helping him to adjust as best he could to their new life. It was a task she had been failing at more than succeeding lately. But if things worked out, Jessie would be going to college soon and Kelsie would be more alone than she had been in years. She hadn't really given it much thought until...she ran into someone she knew from school. Someone she had been happy to rid her life of long ago and now suddenly seemed...interesting. Still, while it would be nice for something to work out with *anyone*, her main focus was her son.

"I'm truly hoping Brice is a better person for the benefit of Jessie," Kelsie stated firmly before adding with a sly smile, "and if something else happens along the way, who am I to doubt fate?"

Tina gave her a knowing smile but worried for her at the same time.

*****

The rest of her week went by uneventfully. Kelsie was kept busy at work, wrapping up as many projects as possible before the fiscal year ended. With tax season just around the corner, there was plenty to do in preparation for her clients year-end statements so she managed to keep focused on important tasks instead of letting her mind wander in regards to what might be ahead of her at the end of the week.

Through the balance of their coffee meetings that week, Kelsie couldn't help but smile at Tina each morning as her friend tried to discreetly watch every person who came into the shop to see if she could spy the man she had met all-too-briefly on Tuesday. Kelsie noted that Tina was as interested in running into him again as she was in running into Brice. Both women wanted to know more about the men who had suddenly been thrust into their lives.

When Saturday finally arrived, Kelsie was up and ready to leave before she realized Brice hadn't set a time for her arrival. She was tossing options of what time was appropriate around in her head when a text came through. She smiled as she read the message from Brice.

'See you at 10:00'.

She wondered if it was a sign that they both came up with the same dilemma at the same time. *Oh stop acting like a high school girl!* she scolded herself. *Focus your thoughts on Jessie!*

Just before 9:00, Kelsie started her journey to Redemption. Traffic was heavier than she expected so she was glad she had left herself extra time. She thought about the holiday shoppers she was passing as they were out finding bargains and fulfilling wish-lists. The only thing she wanted for Christmas was her son back. Not just physically but mentally. She desperately wanted him to get back to being the fun, outgoing young man he was before their lives took a drastic turn.

As she turned into the parking lot of her destination, she checked the time, only to realize she was 5 minutes early. She figured that was reasonable. After all, a boss once told her if she wasn't 5 minutes early to anywhere she needed to be then she was 5 minutes late!

She appreciated the bright, clear sky and seasonable chill in the air as she got out of her car and walked to the center's main entrance. Along her way, she noticed plenty of activity around the barn with a steady stream of people coming out of the main building and the bunk houses as well. But she didn't see Jessie anywhere. Suddenly, panic started to rise up within her. What if he found out she was coming and didn't want to see her? What if Brice was pulling some juvenile high school trick? Her mind was reeling with crazy thoughts as she spied Brice and Jessie coming out of the center and let out a huge sigh of relief.

She quickened her pace and upon catching up to them, gave Jessie an embarrassingly long hug. "Hi honey! I'm so happy to see you!"

Jessie's reaction to seeing his mother was far less enthusiastic than she had hoped for. "Hey Mom," was all he uttered as he barely hugged her.

"Glad you could make it today," Brice said while smiling at Kelsie as he tried to help her through the awkward moment.

"I'm happy to be here." Kelsie hoped her embarrassment didn't show. She figured this wasn't the first time Brice had seen a similar situation but that didn't make it any more bearable for her. She turned to Jessie, who was staring at the stables, seemingly totally disconnected from what was going on around him. "How's it going so far?"

Jessie simply shrugged, then looked at the ground, kicking an invisible stone.

Brice chimed in once again. "So far, so good. Jessie's learning his way around, getting to know people here, learning the routine and getting acquainted with Bailey."

"Bailey?" Kelsie asked.

Brice intentionally remained quiet. He wanted Jessie to engage. After an awkward period of silence, Jessie finally spoke.

"That's the name of the horse I'm taking care of," he said quietly.

Kelsie was thankful to hear him say something, anything. "Well that sounds like fun. I'd like to meet him..or her. That's a great name for a horse." She was at a loss for the right thing to say as words stumbled from her lips.

And Jessie's response clearly informed her she hadn't hit upon the right words yet. "Bailey's a stallion. And it's not supposed to be fun Mom. It's work." He paused for a moment, trying to relax the tone in his voice a bit. "But he's pretty cool. At least he doesn't give me a hard time about anything."

Kelsie looked briefly at Brice, whose expression didn't show any surprise.

"Well, I'm certainly not here to give you a hard time about anything. I just want to see how you're doing, make sure you're OK."

The edge found its way back to Jessie's voice. "I'm fine Mom! Isn't that why you brought me here. To be safe...and out of the way?!"

Kelsie felt a stab in her heart. Obviously he felt she had dumped him at Redemption, which was exactly what she *didn't* want him to think, because it couldn't have been father from the truth. But he clearly needed a dose of reality.

"You weren't in the way! Why would you say that? All along I've only wanted what's best for you. With everything that's happened, I need you more than ever. I need you to be OK, I need you to talk to me, I need you to be the man I know you can be. But instead of all that, you're here because of your behavior, which is anything *but* how a responsible young man should be acting. And if you recall, the judge wanted to give you one more chance. You're lucky she was feeling generous. Otherwise, you'd be in some sort of institution until you're 18 or older! I know you don't want that and I certainly don't want that either. But you keep doing things that are so unlike you. Destructive things, to others and to yourself. And I don't know why. It's like you are trying to push everyone away." She paused and looked at her son with tears welling in her eyes. "You have to know that I want you home more than anything! I miss you."

Kelsie stopped speaking, wondering if she had said too much. Or maybe she hadn't said enough, either at that moment or in the past. She was at her wits end. And desperate.

Jessie looked at the ground, standing perfectly still. He wasn't sure how to react. He wanted to scream. He wanted to run far away. He wanted to hug his mother more than ever. He wanted to feel her comforting arms enveloping him, in the protective way only a mother's arms can manage. He wanted to be anywhere but where he was. Far too many conflicting thoughts were running through his mind. He just wanted to escape.

Brice had a strong sense of what was happening with both of the people standing with him. He had seen similar situations play out before him time and time again. The small details may be different but the concept was the same. Teens think their parents can never understand their dilemma and parents forget what it's like to be a confused teenager. He decided it was best to defuse the situation before something was said that couldn't be unsaid.

"Hey Jessie, why don't you go check on Bailey? I'll catch up with you in a bit."

Jessie didn't need to be given an out from the situation twice. He instantly took off for the stables, seemingly before Brice had even finished speaking.

Kelsie watched him running away from her. "I haven't seen him move that fast in…forever. Am I that bad of a mother he should be so anxious to get away from me?" The sadness in her voice spoke volumes.

"Trust me, it's not you." Brice's voice had a reassuring tone that surprised her. "It's an unfortunate but necessary part of the process. He's starting to realize some things but can't quite figure out how all the pieces go together."

Kelsie gave him a puzzled look.

"What you just said very likely sparked a realization in him. There's a lot going on inside his head and teenagers often don't have the perspective to figure out how to deal with everything they are trying to process. So that's what I need to help him with."

"Maybe I said too much."

"I don't think so. But some of the things you said may have embarrassed him a bit."

Kelsie was flustered. "That definitely was not my intention."

"I know. But it's OK." His reassuring tone, which initially had caught Kelsie off-guard, continued. "Even though deep down he knows it, sometimes hearing someone articulate a person's failures helps them to realize just how much they have stumbled and that they are responsible for their actions and therefore the consequences of those actions. They are the reason he's here, not you. He got here all by himself. He's realizing that now but he needs help figuring out why he's doing the things that landed him here."

"Maybe I shouldn't have come so soon."

"I'm glad you did. Jessie needed to hear what you had to say. It helps when someone you know and trust...and who you know loves you... tells you something. It's hard to hear the truth sometimes. But it's necessary. It'll help in the end."

Kelsie looked towards the stables. "I pray you're right. I don't seem to be able to say anything right these days and I just unloaded on him like never before. I feel terrible about that but, if it helps in the end, I guess it'll be worth it."

"Well, I'm the professional after all, so believe me when I say this will help." Brice smiled as he turned towards Kelsie. "Like the truth you told me the other day."

She shot him a puzzled expression.

"You reminded me of a time in my life I had managed to whitewash over in my memory. It helped me to realize I owe you an apology. Or at least, an explanation. And since I set aside an hour for your visit with Jessie, how about I buy you a cup of coffee?"

Kelsie flashed a slight smile of appreciation at Brice's attempt to lighten her heavy mood. Completely frazzled by what had occurred, she was in no rush to get back in the car and drive home. "I think I'll take you up on that."

As Brice held the door to the dining hall open for her, Kelsie entered into a room that was nothing like what she had imagined. She had fully expected to see something akin to her old high school cafeteria. But instead of rectangular tables with the most uncomfortable seats in the world attached to them, her eyes fell upon round tables that could accommodate up to 8 people easily with comfortable looking chairs at each one. Colorful yet tasteful curtains were pulled open at each window and set against walls colored in warm light beige tones. Live plants were strategically placed throughout the area and artwork, most likely produced by past residents of the facility, covered the walls. While her imagination served her something cold and severe, she was pleasantly surprised by the reality of the bright, inviting room.

Breakfast time was over so Brice easily found a place the two of them could sit and converse privately. As Kelsie got settled into a surprisingly soft chair, Brice went to get coffee.

"Cream but no sugar please," Kelsie responded as he inquired how she took her morning brew. He quickly prepared their drinks, then sat down opposite his guest.

He could see she was still replaying her conversation with Jessie over in her head. Or should it be classified more as a lecture? "Don't beat yourself up," he advised. "He needed a dose of reality and he got it. Worst thing you can do for someone in his situation is white-wash the trouble they are in."

Kelsie's mood was starting to turn sour. "Maybe I really did come too soon."

"I don't think so," Brice reassured her. "He's not the only person who's being affected by what he's been doing so he needed to hear what you said. But he also needed a way out of the conversation. That's why I suggested he go to the stables. It'll give him time to think while everything that was said is still fresh in his head."

Kelsie nodded absentmindedly as she stared into her cup. Suddenly, she came back to the moment. "Can I ask you something personal?"

"I don't see why not," Brice replied, hoping his reply didn't turn out to be a mistake. She knew plenty of things about him that could lead to an uncomfortable conversation. "I can always refuse to answer on the grounds it might incriminate me." He flashed her a slightly nervous smile.

"What happened our senior year? I don't recall seeing you around much." She gestured around the room. "But I can only assume you graduated or you wouldn't be here."

Brice wasn't happy with her question but he also wasn't surprised. "Let's just say there were issues in my home life which, at the start of senior year, required a sudden change of address."

"Most of us assumed you went to live with your mother."

"No, she didn't want anything to do with us. It was if she had fallen off the face of the earth. Or she imagined we had."

She thought his statement explained a few things. If he was to be believed, at a time he probably needed his mother the most, she apparently hadn't any inclination towards being in his life. The thought saddened her. "So you dropped out of school?"

"Not exactly."

Brice contemplated for several moments how many details of his youthful years he should share with her, finally deciding she should know it all: the good; the bad and the ugly. He tried to keep it light as he described his youth, even though it was anything but an easy time in his life. However, he knew he was failing miserably as he spoke.

"Believe it or not, I didn't grow up in a stable environment like you did. My mom left when my brother and I were pretty young. Couldn't really blame her, except that she left us with a dad that was…let's say…not very patient…or understanding…with anybody. He ended up getting into trouble with some guys. Owed them money or something. Anyway, we had to leave town pretty quickly one night right after senior year started. I finished out the school year far away from where I started it."

Brice paused for a moment as Kelsie watched him. To her, he seemed surprisingly calm telling her something only a few people might know. She was appreciating his honesty.

He took a gulp of his coffee before continuing. "Anyway, once I could get away from him, I

got as far away as I could. Then I decided I didn't want to be a screw-up like him so I went to school to be a counselor. Next thing I know, here I am, talking to an old classmate while trying to help as many kids as I can to not be like I was." His smile seemed genuine, if a bit troubled.

Kelsie was silent. She never had a clue what his situation was like when they were in school. She couldn't recall any rumors or behavior that would indicate a problem at Brice's home but she pondered what might have happened if a teacher had taken an interest in investigating Brice's home situation. Knowing what was going on there might have explained, and helped, a lot. Kelsie had tried not to give him much thought back then and most likely wouldn't have known what signs to look for, nor would she have cared to do so. That's what school administrators were supposed to do. She had actually been thankful he seemingly disappeared for their senior year. By then, his presence had ceased to be at all amusing or attractive, no matter how much she might have thought otherwise earlier.

"I'm sorry you had a rough start in life." She truly felt bad for him. "But I'm thankful you turned things around."

They sat in silence for awhile. Kelsie was interested in knowing more details but she knew the time was not right for digging into that conversation.

Finally, Brice spoke up. "Can I ask you about Jessie's father?"

Kelsie was a bit surprised by his question. After all, the details he likely needed to know were in the file he claimed to have carefully examined before Jessie's arrival. But she sensed he might be looking for information that really wouldn't translate well to a sheet of paper in a manila folder.

"What would you like to know?" She was willing to talk about anything if there was a chance it might help her son. Perhaps knowing a detail not covered in Jessie's file could make a difference.

"I'm assuming life at home was good while he was alive."

"It was very good." Kelsie smiled. It had been a while since she thought about how her life had been not that long ago. "Steve was a great husband and father. He and Jessie were very close, certainly closer than most sons seem to be with their fathers these days. I was always thankful they had such a great relationship."

"And I'm assuming Jessie started to change after his father passed." She nodded.

"Would you mind telling me what happened?"

She started to absentmindedly swirl the coffee in her cup. Kelsie hadn't talked about all that had happened in quite some time but knew to do so could be for Jessie's benefit so she took a deep breath and recounted the all-too-recent events. "Steve started feeling ill. Nothing too drastic at first but he couldn't seem to get back to normal. He just wasn't able to shake the fatigue he was feeling and it was getting worse. Long story short, he eventually went to a specialist and by the time we found out it was pancreatic cancer, there wasn't anything they could do." She paused and let out a deep, slow sigh. "He went downhill fast. We only had six months with him once we knew what was wrong." Kelsie didn't want to go into any further details. The memory of losing her first and only love was still fresh and painful.

Brice could see the sadness in her eyes. "I'm really sorry Kel."

Kelsie looked up from the steady stare she held on her coffee cup with a tear in her eye. "That's what Steve used to call me."

"Well, don't I feel like a fool."

"Please don't. It's OK. It's actually nice to hear again," she said with a sheepish smile.

Brice felt awful. He hadn't wanted to make her feel bad. He simply wanted to get some background on Jessie's situation but instead, he had managed to make a woman who was already sad, sadder.

He wasn't certain he should continue but he had to know more to potentially help his newest charge so he pressed a bit further. "Jessie knew his father was dying, right?"

"Absolutely. We didn't hide anything from him once we knew. Steve and I wanted Jessie to have as much time with his father as possible. And we thought it would be worse if he didn't know what was ahead."

"Definitely the right move." Brice had seen the affect of parents keeping things from their kids, usually regarding a potential divorce, and knew all too well that it was never a smart move to try and hide important things from the kids who would be directly affected by the results. "Children are usually more in touch with what's going on around them than parents want to admit. How hard did he take the news initially?"

"Badly," Kelsie admitted. "But we expected that and both worked hard to make sure the time we had left together wasn't full of nothing but sadness. Believe it or not, we managed to have some good times in the midst of devastation. I think they became even closer during that time."

Brice was taking in as much information as possible as Kelsie continued to recall Jessie's last months with his father.

"They did things together as much as they could and they talked all the time. I'm not sure what about but I'm really thankful Jessie had that time with his father."

"So how soon after Jessie's father died did he start to change?"

"Pretty quickly. At first, he got very quiet. He would go for days without saying or doing much of anything. I sorta figured that was normal. But then he started acting out at school, getting into trouble with teachers, cutting classes. Then he dropped out of band, which was his favorite class, and it started to get worse. Shoplifting, vandalism, things that told me he was shouting out for attention. And I was giving him as much as I could, spending as much time with him as possible, even though he wasn't telling me anything. I probably should have taken him to a shrink or something but I was going through the mourning process too and I probably wasn't paying as much attention as I should have to all the signs. I guess I didn't want to admit to myself that something was wrong." She got quiet as she looked up at Brice. "I honestly didn't know what to do. It's been a very tough period for us both."

Brice wanted to instinctively reach across the table and place a comforting hand on Kelsie's but resisted the urge. He had heard stories similar to Kelsie's before but he felt especially affected by hers.

"Even though it wasn't easy," Kelsie continued. "I got through the loss and I've adjusted to life without Steve, as difficult as it was to do so."

"You really are doing amazingly well," Brice assured her.

"But I know Jessie's still having a terrible time with it all."

"Has he ever talked about losing his father?"

"Not really. I figured it was too painful for him and I've been afraid that if I push him to talk about the fact that his father is gone, it could make things worse."

Brice nodded. "So there is nothing in his life to potentially fill the void left by his father's passing?"

Kelsie shook her head slowly.

"And he's lost interest in things he previously enjoyed." It was a statement instead of a question because Brice intuitively knew what Kelsie's response would be.

Kelsie nodded.

Brice started to formulate a plan on how he was going to approach Jessie. "Well, please know that I'm going to do everything I can to help him figure things out. I truly want to help him; to help you both."

Kelsie looked at Brice with pleading eyes. "Thank you. I'm counting on you to help him get back to being the person I know he is deep down inside. He's all I have left." She could feel tears welling up in her eyes and desperately hoped one wouldn't fall down her cheek. She felt it would make her look even more pathetic and she wasn't looking for sympathy.

But then the tear fell.

Brice reached into his pocket for a handkerchief. He had carried clean ones ever since his first day at Redemption, when he had met a parent that was a pitiful, sobbing mess and he had nothing to catch the steady flow of tears that seemed to go on forever. Since then, he often had to pull one out for parents or teens since sometimes a good cry was the best way to break through all the noise. He hadn't thought today would be a day he'd need it but, unfortunately, it was.

Chapter Eight

Brice hadn't slept well. Something about Jessie was literally keeping him up at night. But he wasn't sure if it was Jessie or his mother robbing him of sleep. Seeing Kelsie again stirred up memories that he had managed to avoid for quite some time. His youth had been tumultuous, having wasted much of it with his antics. Over the years, he had managed to successfully avoid thinking about the negative effect his mis-spent youth had had on others. But seeing an old classmate vividly reminded him of the fact that what he had considered fun at the time was much less so for the people around him. Given the opportunity, he would apologize to many of those individuals; his former best friend in particular.

He was starting to realize that the one disadvantage of putting bad memories behind was when they crept back into his life, they were all that much more difficult to deal with as he questioned the choices he'd made along the way. Choices made that had affected so many.

His youth was made difficult by his father. That was a simple fact. The man was a petty criminal whose wife had the good sense to leave him early in their marriage. In fact, Brice was only two and his brother four when they were left in the "care" of their father. He could never figure out how she seemed to so easily put her family behind her. He rarely saw her when he was a child and by the time he had grown up enough to start following in his father's footsteps, she had a new man in her life and a new child to look after. In adulthood, Brice had no contact with his mother or his half-sister and that was fine by him. They never showed an interest in him, even after he straightened out his life, so he had decided long ago not to waste his energy on people who obviously didn't care about him.

Like father; like son. Brice started showing a certain aptitude for screwing up his life at an early age. Without a proper role model at home, he had no way of knowing right from wrong. He started acting out at school to get attention and it worked. At first, he enjoyed being the fun kid in school, even if it got him sent to the principal's office more times than anyone else in the entire school. By a lot! And when his teachers reached a breaking point and could no longer deal with his disruptions, a parent/teacher conference would be called but it never helped alleviate the situation, mostly because of his father's blatant disinterest in changing his parenting style, if it could actually be called "parenting".

Eventually, Brice was no longer being the class-clown for fun. He became rebellious towards authority figures at school instead of realizing they were exactly what he needed in his life. Without rules and consequences, his life became aimless as he started down a whole different, potentially more perilous path. When his father burst through the door of their double-wide late one evening and announced they were leaving town, Brice wasn't surprised. He knew his father had been hanging with shady characters but it didn't bother him. They were fun and treated him more like family than his own.

The hasty exit made with his father and brother came in time for Brice to avoid any serious consequences from his own actions. But even in his youthful naivety, he had often wished he had been just a little older when his father suddenly relocated the family so he wouldn't have had to go with him. But his idiotic old man had managed to piss off the wrong people and if they hadn't left, something bad would have happened, which might have been a relief to all who knew them.

As time passed and booze ultimately became his old man's undoing, Brice was thankful that a stranger took pity on him and helped to steer him in the right direction since, at the time, he was woefully unprepared to support himself in the real world. If the chance meeting had never taken place, Brice's life would have been as wasted as his father's. He never spent time reflecting on his younger years after he left the man who put him into the world passed out on a stained couch in the disgusting pit where they lived.

Except when he was forced to do so. With Jessie's arrival, which included the presence of a person from his past, Brice had been forced to look back, to relive memories long buried. But maybe there was something in his past that could help his newest arrival, although he was struggling to relate anything from his past to Jessie's situation since other than losing their fathers, his past was nothing like Jessie's. Even their losses weren't relatable. He had walked away from his father and from the sound of things, Jessie would never have dreamed of doing such a thing. He had no reason to.

Brice was, in a way, envious of Jessie's situation. He would have appreciated having a father like Jessie's, knowing in his heart it would have been better for him to have had a great dad for a short period of time rather than the disaster of a father he had for far too long. Parental influences carry more weight through a person's lifetime than most people are aware of so a positive influence on a young person, even for a short period, can hold long-term value. He needed to help Jessie realize that, even though he only had his father in his life for a brief period, the relationship was something he needed to hold onto. And cherish. Jessie needed to understand that he should lean on the memories he had of his father, not rail against all that he had been taught. If he could get Jessie to realize the long-term value of the relationship he enjoyed with his father and the fact that his father's wisdom could still help to guide him through life, Brice felt certain he could make a real difference in Jessie's future, undoubtedly making it brighter.

As Brice sat in his office contemplating his dilemma, Jessie walked in and flopped onto a chair without saying a word.

Brice snapped from his brooding memories. "Good morning Jessie." He was purposely overly cheerful, partly to get out from under the ill mood that was about to overtake him but also in the hope of being able to illicit some sort of response, or the tiniest bit of conversation, from Jessie.

True to form to that point, Jessie sat in the chair without engaging in any amount of conversation, staring at the floor.

"It's pretty clear you don't want to be here," Brice continued, "because I'm sure you think our meetings are a waste of time and nothing will be solved by talking with me."

Jessie continued to sit in silence, moving his fixation to some invisible thing on the table in front of him.

"I can guarantee you that talking to me will help more than you can possibly imagine."

Jessie looked up at Brice for a moment, then returned his stare to…whatever.

Brice pushed a little bit more. "Look, you've been through a lot. I know your father dying was quite a blow to you and the life you knew, when all three of you were together, living as a solid family." Brice paused a moment. "Do you want to talk about that?"

They sat in silence for over a minute. Finally, Jessie quietly, hesitantly broke his abstinence from speaking while still staring at the table. "What good will it do?"

Quietly, Brice responded. "You'll be surprised."

"I'll be surprised if I ever want to talk about it." Jessie started to get agitated. "He died and no amount of talking about it will change that fact."

Brice knew he had to tread carefully. He was relieved Jessie was talking but sensed the young man was on the verge of shutting down completely if he didn't take great care in choosing his words. Jessie's body language spoke volumes. "But talking about it might help you to process everything that's happened. And processing the tragedy is an important first step in getting your life back. Isn't that what you want?"

Silence fell over the room again as Brice worried he had pushed too much.

With a slight quiver in his voice, Jessie finally spoke again, quietly. "What's the use in getting my life back if I'm sad all the time?"

"That's a valid question. But it's very likely that, if you get your life back, you won't be sad all the time."

Silence.

"I imagine you're a bit angry as well."

"Yeah I'm angry!" Jessie snapped. "Why did he have to die? Why did we have to lose him?" The frustration was apparent in his voice as it became more forceful.

Brice replied softly. "I'm sorry Jessie, I don't have an answer for you. I truly wish I did."

"Thought you had all the answers."

"Sorry to disappoint."

"So what's the sense in talking about it?"

"To see if we can find the answers you need together. Speaking out loud about what's going through you mind can help to make sense of things. There is a reason for everything that happens in our lives."

Jessie looked squarely at Brice. "In that case, I'd like to know why I don't have a dad anymore."

"I think you're looking at it wrong. You still have a dad, Jessie. He's just not physically here with you any longer. But the things that he taught you, the things you talked about, the things you did together, that's what keeps your father alive. He's with you every moment of every day, in your memory and in your heart."

Jessie's expression reflected a mixture of confusion and…hope.

"It may be hard to comprehend but our lives are really just made up of moments in time. Some moments are better than others and we have the ability to determine what we want to remember and what we want to forget. Maybe you've forgotten your dad a bit. Not because you want to, but because you're angry he isn't here with you anymore. You think you can't seek his advice on things you don't understand, that he can't help you to navigate your way through life. But you actually can talk to him about what you're going through and he can still help you."

Jessie looked more confused than ever as Brice continued to explain his thought.

"Remember how I said that talking about things can help?"

Jessie nodded slowly.

"Saying our thoughts out loud is helpful in many different ways. If we are confused or upset about something, verbalizing the details can help put things into perspective. And with perspective, we can often arrive at a solution to whatever dilemma exists."

Brice paused to let his words resonate for a moment. "Does that make sense?"

Jessie considered Brice's comments for several moments, then nodded.

"So if you have something you want to say to your dad, or ask your dad, do it. Tell him the details of what's bothering you, speak them out loud. Even if you can't talk *with* him, you can talk *to* him and gain clarity from it just by speaking what you're thinking. And believe me, that clarity will help you. You can share good things, bad things, confusing things, anything you want to get off your chest."

Brice let his words sink in before he continued. "Look, there are a lot of things that happen in our lives which we don't understand. We don't know why they happen. We don't know when they'll happen. But the one thing we do know is that, whatever happens, we need to be resilient. Your father passing away so young doesn't make sense. But if you aren't resilient and don't carry on the way he would want you to, remembering everything he taught you, the loss is in vain."

Jessie stared out the office window. The activity outside seemed like it was a thousand miles away. He heard what Brice was saying but it was difficult for him to fully comprehend what he meant. As he sat absentmindedly staring out the window, he felt that, at least, it might make things a bit easier if he concentrated on good things instead of bad. He had lots of great memories of his father. But they had been clouded by memories of him during his last few months. Seeing his father become weak, thin, pale and sicker each day towards the end wasn't a memory that Jessie wanted. But lately, that seemed to be all he could recall, which made him angry. He desperately wanted to remember the good things about his father.

As he watched Jessie, Brice felt there was a chance that what he had said got through. He hoped one more thought would cement something in Jessie that could help.

"Remembering the positive things about him will help to lessen the pain. That's how we keep ourselves thinking straight when dealing with losses like these, by remembering the wonderful things about someone we love. It's much healthier than dwelling on the loss, which is easily done but can ultimately be destructive. But you need to understand that the pain will never go away. And it shouldn't. Because the pain of losing someone close to us helps to remind us that we need to live our lives to the fullest every day and never waste a moment of the time we have in this life. It's a precious gift not to be taken for granted. It sounds like your father never forgot that fact. And hopefully he passed that understanding on to you. He's literally in your blood, he's part of you. So don't ever forget that he's always with you. And don't forget the wisdom he left with you."

Brice stopped talking, knowing he'd filled Jessie's mind with much that he needed to consider. He didn't want to risk overload.

Jessie sat in silence for several moments as he tried to process what Brice had told him. It made sense. Jessie loved his father and had many happy memories of him. But he didn't know if he'd be able to banish the overwhelming sadness he constantly felt and replace it with good memories, as Brice had suggested. He had to have time to think. He needed space.

Brice looked at his watch. After their intense conversation, he felt the only further help he could provide Jessie was time to process everything that had been said. He knew it would be best to end the session early. "Why don't you go check on Bailey? We can talk more later."

Jessie didn't need to be told twice. He quietly got up, left the office and went to his room to get his coat.

***

Outside in the fresh, crisp cold air, Jessie felt…a little less anxious. He knew that Brice was trying to help him. But what he was having trouble understanding was how his father's death was connected to everything else he was going through. He understood his anger was based in something that no one had control over. But he wasn't sure about everything Brice had told him. Was talking to his dead father really the answer? He had to think about that. But one thing he was sure about was the fact he needed help to stay out of jail. Or whatever equivalent possibly awaited him. So he needed to make an effort.

He started walking with no clear direction in mind. But before he realized it, he was headed towards the stables. As he approached, the ever present activity that always seemed to revolve around the building was in full vigor as he made his was inside.

Bailey was standing in his stall, his backside nestled in one corner. As Jessie entered, he grabbed a handful of oats and, without thinking, grabbed the brush sitting on the small shelf near the stall entrance. As he held the oats to the horse's mouth, he felt its lips nibbling at his hand as the oats were vigorously gobbled up. "You really like these things, don't cha boy?" he murmured.

Slowly, gently, he started to brush the long, strong neck as he whispered into Bailey's ear. "Thanks for not asking any more from me than a handful of oats and a good brushing. Brice thinks I should be talking to my dad. I don't know if that makes sense." He paused as he was struck by the irony. "But then, I'm talking to you so maybe it's not a stupid idea after all."

Bailey's ear twitched as Jessie spoke. He knew the horse didn't understand anything he was saying but he kept on talking about his dad, his situation and all that he had managed to screw up lately, all the while brushing and patting the animal.

"You're lucky. You don't have to deal with this kinda crap. Your life is simple. Wish mine still was. It was nice when all I had to worry about was what I was gonna do with my dad on the weekend. Now I gotta worry about mom and fixing the stuff I've done and…" His voice trailed off as his thoughts became too confused for him to speak them out loud. He tried to calm the noise in his head as he continued to brush Bailey.

April walked past the stall. "Hi Jessie", she called out.

No response came.

She popped her head over the stall wall. "You not speaking to me?"

He hadn't even noticed her initial greeting. He snapped out of his funk long enough to say, "Hi."

"You OK?" she asked with genuine concern.

He didn't look up as he responded. "I wish people would stop asking me that!"

"Sorry, didn't mean to piss you off. I just wanted to make sure you're OK." She wasn't quite sure what to make of their encounter so far.

Jessie suddenly felt worse for snapping at her since she was someone he'd like to have as a friend when his time at Redemption was finished. "I didn't mean you," he said sheepishly. "Actually, I didn't mean what I said at all. I just wish people would stop trying to get me to talk about what's bugging me. Talking about it isn't going to change anything!" His intense tone reflected the frustration he felt.

"But I think that talking about what's going on with you is how you get the help you need."

"I don't need help!" he snapped. "I just need people to leave me alone."

At the risk of possibly making things worse, April explained herself. "I don't mean that you need *help*. I mean that it's good to talk to someone so they can *help* you to figure things out. I don't think it's good to keep everything bottled up inside."

Jessie started pacing in Bailey's stall as the horse stood in the corner, sensing his anxiety. "I just want people to leave me alone. No one understands what I'm going through."

"But that's probably why Brice wants you to talk, so he can know you, know what you're going through, know what's upsetting you. No one can know you until you let them."

"Maybe I don't want anyone to know me."

"That silly. You've built a wall around yourself, trying to insulate yourself from everyone and everything. But it's OK to let others in. They only want to help." April stared at Jessie with concern in her gaze, which he never noticed.

Jessie also never noticed Bailey getting more anxious, staying close to the corner while steadily stomping his right hoof.

"You're starting to sound like one of them."

"Is that such a bad thing?"

Jessie paced a bit more, then suddenly stopped to consider her query. As he stood still, so did Bailey.

April continued. "I'm speaking from experience. I used to be a lot like you. Wouldn't talk to anyone, didn't want to do anything. I just wanted to be left alone."

"Why?"

His simple question made April pause. She didn't want to get into that particular conversation at that particular moment. "I had my reasons."

"Oh, so you want me to talk but you don't have to?"

She shot him a snarky look combined with a slight smile.

Jessie looked as her quizzically. "So what changed? You seem pretty cool to me."

Her smile grew slowly as she responded. "I talked to someone."

Jessie stared at her in silence. It was a simple response that he should have expected. She made it sound so easy. But to him, it simply wasn't.

Bailey slowly moved from the corner of the stall to where Jessie stood, his nose eventually nudging Jessie's shoulder, as if the animal was saying, 'it'll be OK'.

He reached around and started scratching Bailey's long snout, running his forefinger around the white patch in the middle as he turned to stare the animal in the eye.

April smiled in surprise at the scene before her. "Looks like Bailey may have finally taken to someone. You two might be kindred, misunderstood spirits."

The horse did appear to be trusting him all of the sudden. It was the first time Bailey had approached Jessie. Up until then, it was always the other way around, with Jessie needing to approach slowly. Now Bailey did the same to Jessie. What the reason for the breakthrough was, Jessie didn't know. But he liked the feeling that he had apparently done something that informed the horse he was a person who could be trusted.

As April saddled Beau, she called over her shoulder. "I'm getting ready to go for a ride. Wanna join us?"

"I don't know how to ride," he stated matter-of-factly.

"It's not that tough. I can teach you…if you'll *let* me."

Jessie cracked a slight smile at the sarcasm thrown his way while April finished saddling Beau. Then she walked into Bailey's stall and grabbed the red plaid blanket hanging over the wooden wall and placed it on Bailey's back. She took it as a good sign that the blanket didn't spook the horse.

"This protects his back from the saddle and, if it was warmer, it would help to absorb the sweat generated by the exertion of the animal being ridden with a heavy leather saddle on its back."

She pointed to a worn saddle straddling the wall next to where the blanket had hung. "Grab that saddle."

Jessie attempted to do as instructed but the heavy, awkward saddle was difficult for him to handle.

"Here, let me show you how to hold it," April offered. She showed him where to hold the back while holding the horn at the front. "Let's put this on his back nice and easy since I don't know how much he's been ridden before now. If he spooks, be ready to get out of his way fast."

They gently placed the saddle over the blanket as Bailey simply stood still, patiently letting April show Jessie how to place the straps around his belly.

"You have to get these straps good and tight." she instructed. "Otherwise the saddle will slip around and you'll be looking at the underside of Bailey as you're riding." She was happy her comment got a chuckle out of Jessie.

After the bit was in place, she showed him how to handle the reins, the leg motions to use when he wanted to horse to move forward and the leg and rein motions needed to stop the noble beast.

"Just remember, if Bailey takes off, your natural instinct will be to squeeze your legs around his body to hang on. But to him, that just means you want him to run faster. So if he takes off, relax your legs and pull back on the reins while saying 'Whoa'."

"I thought that was just what they said in the movies." Jessie was genuinely surprised.

"Sometimes what you see in the movies is real. And don't forget to thank Bailey for putting up with 150 pounds riding around on his back. A nice pat on the neck and a soothing, calm voice will let him know you appreciate him."

With the help of a step-stool, Jessie got into the saddle as April mounted Beau. After a few last minute pointers and a few easy test laps around the corral, April posed the question that made Jessie suddenly question the whole idea of going for a ride.

"You ready?"

"I have no idea," he replied pensively. "But let's give a shot."

"OK, then, nice and slow, until you get the feel for each other. Just follow me."

As they started out towards the field, Jessie leaned over and patted Bailey's neck, then whispered into his ear. "Take it easy on me, OK buddy? We'll talk more later."

Chapter Nine

It was rare when a day wrapped up early for Brice but he was always thankful when it happened. After meeting with Jessie in the morning, he caught up on paperwork, checked in with some of the other counselors on their program participants and had an early dinner. As he sat in his living area, he started to reflect on his past. He looked around at the meager furnishings in his apartment. The place was neat and clean but it wasn't hard to keep it that way. He needed order in his life and the size of his dwelling easily allowed him to have that. Aside from his slightly extravagant stereo system, his comfortable chair, loveseat, small coffee table and television did not make for a lot of upkeep. The tiny eat-in kitchen was functional but nothing more. And the single bedroom contained nothing more than what was needed for a good night's sleep. It suited Brice just fine that his home was free of things like family photos, artwork that had been printed by the thousands and little things sitting on shelves or tables, what some people thought of as things that give a home the "personal touch". He didn't need to be surrounded by clutter nor did he need photos of family members staring at him every day, reminding him of darker times.

His current surroundings were more than sufficient for him alone and alone was just what he wanted to be. But since Kelsie had popped up, he found himself thinking more and more about some of the less savory aspects of his past. He had managed to bury a lot of memories but he knew full-well that burying the past wasn't the best way to deal with it. So much had changed in his life, thankfully for the better. But that didn't change what went before.

When his father's past finally caught up with him, Brice took it as his "fork in the road" moment.

While his father paid for his transgressions in one way or another, Brice had an awakening that moved him toward a better life. But he had a few loose ends in his past that he never wrapped up, mostly centered around people he knew during his teenage years. Kelsie was certainly part of that group. The more he remembered about her, the more he recalled how he had felt about her back then. That is, if he had had the opportunity to feel anything about her. Or anyone. He always knew she was too good for him. She came from an upper middle-class family and he most certainly did not. She had refinement which he clearly didn't. She worked hard to do well in school and he did anything but. He hadn't thought about any of this in years. He hadn't thought about Bill in years either. For quite some time, his thoughts had been that it was best for some things to be left in the past, not to be dwelled upon. Now he wasn't so sure.

Before he allowed himself to wallow in the past for too long, he grabbed the TV remote and started flipping through channels, not really seeing anything that came across the screen. As he sat in his chair, he could feel his phone digging into his thigh. He removed it from his pocket and set it on the coffee table but quickly picked it up again, curiously filled with the urge to make a phone call. To whom, he didn't know. The realization that he had no one to call was jarring to him. He was usually too busy to notice something like this. He looked at his phone for several long moments before punching in a number.

***

Kelsie was on her overstuffed and very comfortable chair in her living room feeling uncertain of what to do. Her evenings were lonelier than ever with Jessie not at home. Even when he was in his room playing video games or in the yard shooting hoops, just knowing he was at the house made her feel like she wasn't alone. With her husband gone and Jessie away, her thoughts wandered, not always to the best of places.

Her head was full of so many doubts concerning how she had handled things since Steve's death. Certainly she was wishing she had done something differently where Jessie was concerned. Looking back, she might have considered sending him for counseling. Would doing so have meant she couldn't handle the situation? That she was weak or a bad parent? But how was she to know the right way to handle the situation? Was there a rule book for dealing with the premature death of your husband? Was there a handbook on how to best handle a teenage son who just lost his father?

After Steve's death, she was constantly barraged with well-wishers asking if she was OK. It never occurred to her that she might have needed help. She thought she had everything under control. But the facts surrounding why she was alone in her house said otherwise. She had always handled any situation that came her way so the thought of failing never entered her mind as she soldiered on alone, trying to help Jessie handle the tremendous loss of his father while at the same time dealing with the tremendous loss of her husband. She knew she had handled it all wrong and would do a lot of things differently if she had to do it all over again. But that was something she *never* wanted to live through again!

She was deep in thought as the sound of her phone startled her. Trying to focus her thoughts, she answered without checking to see who was calling.

"Hello?"

"Hey there," Brice said, happy she picked up.

Kelsie snapped back to reality upon hearing his voice and suddenly panicked. "Is Jessie OK?"

Brice hadn't anticipated that a call from him would immediately trigger her going to a dark thought that something was wrong. "Yes, he's fine, really."

"Oh thank God," a relived Kelsie replied as her heart started to calm in her chest. "I thought maybe he had fallen off of Bailey or something."

"Sorry, didn't mean to scare you. I promise he's doing fine. He's still getting used to the place but he's making progress."

"OK," Kelsie sighed. "Sorry, I don't know why I assumed the worst."

"Probably because it's late in the day and you're getting a call from someone who usually doesn't call you to chat."

"That might have something to do with it." She smiled. "What's up?"

Awkwardly, Brice realized he had no real reason for his call, other than the one he didn't want to mention. He stammered as he chose his words. "I…just wanted to see…how you're doing?"

"That's a good question." She was glad it wasn't a video call so he couldn't see the mixed expression of surprise and delight she was certain shown on her face. "I guess that, under the circumstances, I'm OK."

Kelsie paused for a moment. "Actually, I'm really not. But I guess I could be doing worse. I'm just worried about Jessie. I'm pretty certain I've handled everything completely wrong since Steve's death and now he's paying the price."

"Don't think like that," Brice cautioned. "We all do the best we can in the moment. Most times we get it right; sometimes we don't. But I don't think we're dealing with anything here that can't be fixed."

She thought it was interesting he used the word "we". Did it mean he was simply invested in helping Jessie or did it indicate something else? She couldn't know for sure.

"I hope you're right. I mean, you're the professional so you have to be right, right??" She stumbled through her words like a nervous schoolgirl.

He chuckled at the nervousness he could hear in her voice. "I've got a diploma that says as much!"

She finally took a breath and relaxed, putting her thoughts about the term he used out of her mind. "Well, I would certainly rather have him here with me right now, with the holidays approaching, helping me get ready. I miss the things we like to do together at this time of year. But at least he's in a place that can get him back to me soon. At least, that's my hope."

Brice had heard heartbreak in a parent's voice all too often. But Kelsie's struck him as being particularly sad. "It's my hope as well, believe me."

"I know." She heard true sincerity in his voice and hoped it wasn't just something he turned on for all parents. "But my friend Tina keeps questioning whether or not Redemption is the right place for him."

A twinge of regret came back into Brice's thoughts. "You mean because of me."

"Sorry." Kelsie regretted bringing up her friend's concern. "But she does have strong memories of you during the time we were all in school."

"Tina," Brice repeated the name as he searched his memory once again. "I think I remember her. You two still hang out?"

She laughed. "You sound like the kids you counsel."

"Occupational hazard."

"Yes, Tina and I still "hang out". We've been best friends since second grade!"

"Well, as I recall, she never liked me. And she had good reason not to so I'm certain she's unlikely to believe that I've changed."

"True, especially since she does have specifically strong memories of all the trouble you caused in school like pulling the fire alarms."

"Only on exam days," he laughed.

She smiled as she continued. "And she reminded me the other day of the time you and your friend Bill wrapped the principle's house with toilet paper."

That was a memory Brice had done his best to suppress but figured making light of it could help to ease his current discomfort. "It was so funny to watch his face when he came out and saw everything hanging from his house and trees."

"I'm sure he wasn't entertained. Whatever made you think to do that?"

"I remember my dad telling me that's what they used to do when he was a kid so I thought it would be a great bit of retro mischief. It's weird but we did so much stuff that was a lot worse than wrapping toilet paper around someone's house yet that's what we got dinged for the worst. It wasn't my brightest idea."

"What wasn't a bright idea was using your dad's car as the getaway vehicle. Pretty easy for the cops to find you once principle Evans gave them the license plate number."

Brice chuckled. "Yeah, I shoulda thought that through better. My dad was definitely not happy with me. Neither was Bill."

"We figured that was why you never came back after summer vacation. We thought you had been permanently expelled."

"No, just for the rest of the year, which was almost over anyway. Then we had to leave town so it didn't really affect me." With a twinge of regret, Brice added, "it was the last adventure of 'Brice and Bill'."

"As I recall, you and Bill were pretty tight. Do you two still keep in touch?"

"No, we drifted apart, even before I left. He was pretty mad that our adventurous evening cost him a college scholarship that he was counting on. He really needed it 'cause his family was as broke as mine."

"But you two were inseparable at school."

"Apparently not." This wasn't the conversation he had been hoping for when he dialed Kelsie's number. But then, he didn't really know what kind of conversation he had been expecting.

"I would think he'd be over it by now."

"Like I said, I haven't heard from him since before I left town so who knows."

"So then you don't know that he's doing quite well these days. He's married with two beautiful kids and runs a successful business in town. I run into him every now and then. Seems very happy."

"I'm glad to hear it."

"Maybe he'd like to hear from an old friend."

Brice had thought of his old best friend over the years, his one memory he didn't work to suppress. He'd thought about reaching out to him several times but didn't want to risk stirring up old issues. "Wish I could share your confidence."

"Isn't one of the steps to getting your life back in order making amends to the people who you have wronged in the past?"

"I think you have us confused with AA," Brice chuckled.

"I'm pretty certain the same principles apply."

He considered Kelsie's suggestion for a moment. "You may have a point. I'll give it some thought."

"I'm thinking you should do a bit more than give it some thought, but that's just me." She smiled at the thought of helping the person who was hopefully helping her son.

Brice was struck by the simplicity of Kelsie's suggestion that could go a long way towards healing old wounds. "And I'm thinking you might want to give thought to changing careers. Ever thought about being a counselor?"

"Pretty sure I don't have the qualifications," Kelsie laughed. "Remember that I was the "good-girl" in school." She hoped he didn't take offence.

He laughed. "Too bad. You might have had a real future."

"I'll stick with my numbers and spreadsheets. They never disappoint me."

"To each his own."

"I actually don't know how you do what you do. How do you handle it when kids don't graduate from your program or they go back to their old ways after leaving Redemption?"

"It happens more than I'd like that kids either leave before they are ready or revert back to being a burden on society. But since I look at even one failure as being too many, statistically, most of the kids straighten themselves out before they leave us. And when one doesn't, I just remind myself of all the successes we've had. They outweigh the failures and remind me that it's all worthwhile."

"Seems like a great way to approach things."

"For me, it's pretty much the only way to look at it. A lot of people dwell on negativity and loss. I like to take a more positive approach."

"I hope you can help Jessie to do the same."

"I'm giving it my best shot. We have a ways to go still." Brice's voice turned hopeful. "Are you coming to visit him this weekend?"

"I was wondering if I should." Apprehension clouded her response. "My last visit didn't go as I would have liked."

"Don't worry about that. I think it might be a good idea for you to visit again."

"Is that Jessie's counselor talking or the reformed school bad-boy?" The words fell out of Kelsie's mouth before she could stop them. She meant them in a teasing manner but wasn't sure that's how they were received. She held her breath.

On the other end of the call, Brice smiled. "See you Saturday."

As the call ended, Kelsie stared at her phone as she continued to be surprised by what she had said. But the truth was, she had been thinking about Brice ever since their reunion. And while she was looking forward to seeing Jessie on the weekend, she was looking forward to seeing Brice too.

***

"You awake?"

Jessie heard his roommate's words clearly since he was wide awake as he relived another day at Redemption. His mind as too busy to let sleep invade. It had actually been a decent day so he wasn't certain why he was having trouble sleeping. April hadn't been around all day so he spent much of it with Bailey, eventually deciding to saddle him up and go for a ride, during which he talked incessantly to the animal. He was contemplating why he found it so easy to talk to Bailey and not to anyone else.

"Yeah," he finally replied.

"Can I tell you something?"

"Don't see why not." Jessie thought his roomy was a decent kid. More outgoing than Jessie, they hadn't spent much time together other than when it was lights-out, but he felt they could likely be friends "on the outside". Max was funny and easy to be around. Maybe they would stay in touch.

"I've been missing someone who used to be here. I'm thinking it's someone I'd like to contact when I'm done here, maybe date."

"That's cool." Jessie was wondering if he was starting to feel the same way about someone he had met there as well. "So what's the big deal? Give her a call when you get out."

Max hesitated before correcting Jessie. "Him," he finally whispered.

"OK, him. Call him when you get out."

Max was astounded. Jessie showed absolutely no reaction to a revelation he thought was massively huge. He had built up in his head the moment when he would admit to someone he was gay as being a roof-shaking, earth-quaking moment. And now that he had finally said it…nothing. Not so much as a blip. He was definitely relieved but not really certain everything was understood.

"That's all you have to say?"

"What did you want me to say?"

"I've never told anyone this. I thought you'd be shocked."

"Why?" Jessie replied matter-of-factly. "I mean, I guess I get that it's a big deal for you. And I'm glad you feel comfortable enough to tell me since we don't know each other that well. And maybe that's part of the reason you chose to tell me. But it doesn't really affect me. So to me, it's not a big deal."

"I…." Max had trouble finishing his thought because he was actually relieved Jessie's reaction was a non-reaction. "I thought you'd, I don't know, act like…"

"An idiot? Shocked? Like I want a new roommate?" Jessie popped up in his bed and faced Max on the opposite side of the room, trying to make out his face in the dark. "Look, dude, what you do in your love-life in none of my concern. If you want to date a guy, go for it. It doesn't matter to me. Live your life and be happy."

"Thanks. I appreciate you saying that." Even in the dim light, Max could see sincerity on Jessie's face. "I really never have told anyone this before."

"Not even your parents?"

"They'd be the last people I'd tell first. They won't understand."

Jessie lay back down in his bed. "That sucks. I could tell my dad anything, even something like that." Knowing that made Jessie feel glad and sad at the same time. He truly could talk to his dad about anything. But not anymore. "Guess we should get some sleep."

"Yeah."

Jessie paused. "I'm not, by the way."

"Don't worry," Max laughed softly. "I'm not crushin' on you."

"But if you want my advice, tell your folks. Maybe they'll surprise you. I mean, why wouldn't they want you to be yourself, to be happy? Generally, that's what parents want for their kids. At least, that's my experience."

"You're lucky. But I'll think about it."

"I don't think there is any need to hide yourself from them."

"Maybe you're right." Max hoped he was.

"Besides, they'll figure it out when you bring this guy home to meet them," Jessie laughed.

"His name is Hunter." Max smiled as he stared at the ceiling. "I think that's a great name."

"Hunter and Max. Has a good ring to it."

"Goodnight Jessie."

"Night Max."

Chapter Ten

B rice sat at his desk, staring at his morning coffee…and the calendar. It was Friday, only one day left in the week. And he had been looking forward to the end of the week ever since his call to Kelsie. He realized he was starting to feel like a high school kid, mooning over the popular girl in class, anticipating seeing her in the hall, imagining talking to her after class, maybe being lucky enough that she would agree to go out with him. He was feeling all the things teenagers feel during their school years, when they experience their first crush. Or at least, he imagined these were the feelings they felt, since he never got to experience the more positive aspects of high school. But he had heard this is what it felt like. And he was enjoying the feeling.

He was lost in his teenage thoughts when he noticed that Jessie was sitting on the couch along the wall of his office, having quietly walked in for their morning talk. "Sorry Jessie, I didn't hear you come in."

"No problem. I think I'm a little early." Jessie felt a bit more relaxed but was still guarded when it came to talking with Brice. Or, for that matter, anyone at Redemption. Except April. And Bailey.

"I'll take that as a sign you aren't feeling like our talks aren't the worst thing in the world anymore." Brice flashed a casually disarming smile that caught Jessie off guard as he cracked his own glimmer of a smile. "I see that you are starting to open up to people around here, including April."

"She's cool."

"Glad you made a friend. And you seem to be getting along with Bailey pretty well too."

"He's cool too."

"But you haven't really talked to me about anything."

Jessie looked out the window, watching all the activity that was happening while trying to understand how it was that everyone seemed so sure of where they were going and what they were doing when he wasn't even sure of what he wanted to say to Brice.

"I'm only trying to help you."

Jessie looked at the floor, confused. "So you keep telling me."

Brice thought it was finally time to push Jessie, hoping it would spark conversation and not lead to him shutting down. "I assume you and your dad used to talk about a lot of things, right?" He held his breath slightly, waiting for an indication either way of what would happen.

Jessie knew he had to eventually talk about his father. Ever since Brice had told him his father lived on inside him, he had been thinking about just that. It was a realization that took him by complete surprise. But Brice was right. His father had taught him so much. And Jessie could talk to him about anything. He missed that. A lot.

After what seemed like an eternity to Brice, Jessie simply nodded.

Brice continued cautiously. "You probably talked about things that you wanted to do, things you wanted to know, things that were happening in your life, right?"

Brice wasn't sure his attempt to delve into what he was certain was the source of Jessie's issue was going to work. Sometimes an early positive indication like the nod he received moments prior could go south in a flash. He waited. And finally received another nod.

"So I'm thinking you could talk to him about anything at all."

The nod came a little quicker this time.

"He was most likely the strongest influence in your life."

Jessie thought about Brice's statement. He had never thought about his father in that way. He had always gotten along with both his mother and father and loved them both. But he was closer to his dad and he truly could talk with him about anything. He knew most of his friends weren't fortunate enough to have similar relationships with their fathers.

Brice let his last statement settle in with Jessie for a few moments before continuing. "I think I owe you an apology."

Jessie looked up quizzically.

"I've been telling you ever since you got here that you can talk to me about anything." Brice's expression reflected his genuine regret.

"And now you're telling me I can't?"

"Not at all. You can absolutely talk to me about anything. But, you talked with your dad about all kinds of stuff. And you can do the same here but I don't want you to think..." Brice paused, not wanting to say the obvious, suddenly at a loss for the right words. He took a deep breath before he continued.

"Look, no one will ever take the place of your dad. He was your father and always will be. Nothing is going to change that. Ever. He loved you and you had a great relationship and it totally sucks that he's gone. Believe me, I get that. But staying angry about the fact that he isn't here with you isn't doing you any good. So I want you to understand something. Anything that's going on with you that you want help in figuring out, that's what I'm here for. To listen, to offer advice, to bounce ideas off of, to talk about whatever you want to talk about. I'm here to help you."

Jessie looked at Brice, then looked out the window, then looked at his feet. He wasn't sure of anything at that moment, other than he wanted to get out of there. He wanted to be somewhere that he could think, somewhere that he didn't have to talk. He desperately wanted to be with someone who didn't care about how he had messed things up for himself and his mother. He literally wanted to run away from everything. But he knew he couldn't. His situation had to be dealt with and he knew Brice was trying to help him do just that. But it wasn't working.

Finally, Jessie got up. "I get it. But right now, I gotta take care of Bailey." Then he swiftly slipped out the office door.

Brice looked at the empty doorway of his office and took a deep breath. He wasn't sure if he had made progress or put Jessie back to the frame of mind he had when he first arrived. But he knew he'd find out soon enough.

***

After leaving Brice's office, Jessie went to get his jacket but sat down on his bed instead. He looked at his surroundings and was instantly depressed. *How did I end up here?* he asked himself. But he knew the answer to his own question. The more difficult question was *why?* He knew the actions that landed him where he was, but figuring out what brought about those actions would take more consideration. And he had just left the person tasked with helping him to figure it all out but he hadn't felt he could handle the conversation Brice was headed towards. Which he knew wasn't helping his situation. He only had until Christmas Eve to straighten himself out.

So he sat and tried to figure himself out. He knew he couldn't do it on his own but he had to organize his thoughts so when he and Brice really did have *the conversation,* Jessie would know exactly what he wanted to say.

He was angry his father was no longer with him. That was easy to figure out. But why did he keep acting out in ways he knew would embarrass his dad since they had been embarrassing for his mother...and himself? He didn't know why he couldn't stop himself. He just kept doing things that were out of character. His head was swirling as he found himself rocking back and forth.

He wasn't sure how long he had been sitting there when Max popped his head into their space and saw his roomy rocking back and forth on the edge of his bed. "You OK?"

Jessie became conscious of his manic movement and immediately stopped, slightly embarrassed. "Yeah, just trying to figure out how I got here."

Max sat on the chair next to the bed. "That's easy. You screwed up, just like me."

"You think?"

"Indeed I do,"

"Thanks for the advice doc. Send me a bill." Jessie wasn't really in the mood to get into anything deep with Max.

"Look, it's not easy to open up but you got do it sometime. So do it sooner rather than later so you can have some fun while you're here."

Jessie looked at Max, whose smile was infectious. "You do seem to be having a lot more fun here than anyone would think a sane person would."

"That's because I decided early on I was gonna see if they know their stuff here and I opened up to my counselor. And even though I didn't want to admit or believe it would help, it absolutely did. So now I'm coasting along until my time is up and I get to go home. So I figure, why not start celebrating the holiday early?"

Jessie was jealous and grateful at the same time that Redemption had been able to help Max turns things around. "Glad it worked out for you but I'm not so sure it's all that simple for me."

"Or maybe you're just making it more complicated by over-thinking it. Telling your counselor what's in your head will help."Max nudged Jessie with a smile. "I promise that you're in the right place to straighten things out."

Jessie's mood lifted a bit as he smiled. "You gonna let them straighten you out."

Max let out a hearty laugh. "I never should have told you!"

Jessie smiled at his new friend.

Max got up and grabbed a t-shirt from his dresser drawer. "I've got a pottery class to get to."

"Pottery? Really?" Jessie couldn't imagine him finding anything helpful in making pottery.

Max waved his hands about with a wild look in his eyes. "I'm still in search of a hobby to keep these idle hands busy." Then he became serious as he continued. "Don't worry. I know you're gonna be fine. We're both going to be fine." He winked at Jessie and was off.

Jessie looked at the empty entrance to their room. "Good luck," he said softly. Then he grabbed his jacket and set off in search of something to keep his idle hands busy too. And to hopefully calm his mind.

***

As she came out of Beau's stall, April could see Jessie approaching the stables, seemingly deep in thought. She had been spending more and more time thinking about him. The more she was around him, the more she saw something special in him. While she could do without the sadness within, she felt that would soon give way to something very positive. She was starting to have trouble keeping that opinion and her feelings in check. *Might not be the best time to start something that will be tough to sustain,* she told herself.

As Jessie walked past her without looking her way, April figured he might be in need of a distraction. "Wanna go for a ride?"

Jessie came back to reality at hearing her voice. "Sorry, didn't notice you. Too deep into my head." He continued to walk towards Bailey's stall.

"Hey Mr. Deep-Thinker! You forgot to answer my question."

"Yeah, sorry," Jessie stammered. "Sounds good. But I may need your help making sure the saddle is on secure enough."

"Just give me a shout if you get into trouble," April called out as she prepared Beau for what she hoped would be an even more fun ride, now that she would have company.

Jessie walked into Bailey's stall, softly calling out to him as he approached so as not to startle him. But his eyes didn't quite comprehend the sight he encountered.

"April come quick!" he blurted out. The distress in Jessie's voice was apparent.

As April hurried to the stall, she was slightly panicked. "What's happened?" She could see Jessie was white as a sheet as she approached. When she entered the stall, she immediately comprehended the source of his distress.

On the floor of the stall lay Bailey, quivering, clearly in pain but not making a sound, as if he didn't want to bother anyone. Jessie stood in stunned surprised, seemingly at a loss as to what he should do. He stood transfixed as April moved over to Bailey. She patted his neck and shoulder, then lightly touched his belly, which caused the animal to flinch and raise its head momentarily.

"What's wrong with him?" Panic saturated every word coming from Jessie's mouth.

"He's clearly in pain and his stomach is tender. I don't know enough to be certain but I've seen something like this before. I think he may have colic."

"What's that?"

"An obstruction in his intestine."

"Is it serious?" Jessie was starting to be consumed with worry.

"It can be if it's not treated quickly."

"So what do we do?"

"Call the vet to make sure!" April went over to a phone on the wall that was connected directly to the office in the main building.

When she was done explaining the situation, she hung up and rejoined Jessie at Bailey's side. He was quietly talking to the horse while gently stroking his neck. "Alex is calling the vet we use." April quickly regretted her choice of words and continued talking before Jessie could ask her who "we" is. "Don't panic. If it is colic, it's treatable."

"What do we do now?" He was desperate to make sure Bailey was going to be OK.

"Remain calm. Remember I told you that horses sense our feelings. If you're in a panic, he'll know it. Just keep doing what you're doing. I'll go find Brice."

Jessie knew she was right and tried to calm down for Bailey's sake but struggled to do so. "OK, but hurry back."

"I won't be gone long."

As April started up the hill to the main building, she saw Brice hurrying towards the stable, obviously having been told about Bailey. She admired the fact that Brice cared as much about the animals at the facility as he did about the participants in the program. She turned to head back to the stable as Brice arrived at her side.

"What's happening here?" Brice asked as he entered Bailey's stall. He knelt down and felt the horse's side, which again elicited a flinch from the noble beast.

"How long before the vet gets here?" Jessie pleaded.

"Should be here in 20 minutes. Any idea how long he's been down?

"I walked in here less than 5 minutes ago and he was already on the ground."

"He was up when I came to get Beau," April offered. "I saw his head pop up over the stall wall when I came in. But I didn't really look at him."

As Brice comprehended the details, he decided on a course of action. "OK, well, if it is colic, the best thing is for him to move around so let's try to entice him into standing and walking."

They tried in vain to coax the horse into standing. But Bailey's pain was simply too severe for him to exert any energy, lest the pain increase. So it appeared, at that moment, the only thing they could do was try to remain calm for the horse's sake. And wait for the vet to arrive.

***

The local vet went by the single name of Jackson. He never actually told anyone any other name and hated it whenever someone would refer to him as "Dr. Jackson", "Doctor" or "Mr. Jackson". *Just call me Jackson* was always his response whenever someone referred to him any other way. This quirk was easily overlooked by everyone who came into contact with him once they experienced the ease with which he treated the animals under his care. He seemed to have a sense about them that no one understood but everyone appreciated, especially his patients. More than one person had noted over the years that there was a very good chance Jackson liked animals more than people. His bedside manner with animals was impressive to all who witnessed it so by the time he emerged from the stall, Bailey was up and walking and feeling a bit better. Now Jackson had to deal with the three people anxiously awaiting his report. He would rather spend more time with his patient.

Brice and April leaned on a wall while Jessie paced like a nervous expectant father-to-be. When he saw Jackson, he practically sprang over to him in a single leap. "How is he?"

"It's colic. A mild case, but it's still serious."

"How serious?"

"Anytime an animal has an obstruction in its intestine, it's serious. But, like I said, it's mild. I gave him something for the pain that should also provide him relief." Jackson could see the worry on Jessie's face and flashed him a reassuring smile. "Don't worry. Bailey will be fine."

"What do you think caused it?" April queried.

"Well, most likely he's been eating too many oats."

Jessie didn't understand. "Oats?"

Jackson walked over to a sink and started washing up as he prepared to pack his bag and, hopefully, make a quick exit. "Yup. Too many oats can easily cause this condition and I see a bag of them hanging over there that's half-full." He nodded at the sack Jessie had been grabbing from for days. "They make a great treat but he needs to be fed a limited amount."

Jessie became quiet.

April sensed Jessie's sudden discomfort and chimed in. "What should we do for Bailey, doc?"

Jackson winced but didn't bother correcting her. He would soon be alone in his car, then back at his practice treating the animals in his care. Exactly where he wanted to be. "Make sure he's got plenty of fresh water. And keep him moving. Not constantly, but several times an hour he needs to walk. Just walk. No running. And no oats for a couple days."

"Thank you Jackson," Brice offered. "I'll walk you to your car."

"No need," Jackson proclaimed as he waved his arm towards the group. "Goodbye. Call me if Bailey takes a bad turn." Seemingly very anxious to get away from people, he nearly broke into a sprint as moved towards the parking lot.

Brice peaked in Bailey's stall. "He's looking better so I'll leave him in your hands Jessie. Do what Jackson said and I'll check in with you tomorrow morning. I've got to get back to it." He left the stables without another word, hopeful but somewhat concerned about what tomorrow might bring.

April turned to Jessie to find he was white as a sheet again. "Don't worry. You heard the doc. Bailey's going to be fine."

With panic in his voice, Jessie blurted "I made him sick!" He started pacing, more upset than ever.

"What are you talking about?"

"You heard the doc say that too many oats can cause colic."

April nodded quizzically.

Jessie hesitated. "I've been giving Bailey oats pretty regular. And I gave him two scoops last night with his dinner."

"Why?"

"Because he really likes them. A lot!" He looked to be on the edge of tears. "I never thought they might be bad for him."

"Jessie, I told you that oats are a *treat* for horses, not a main food. They don't need more than one or two small handfuls a day."

"Yeah but I didn't know that. I never knew anything like this could happen! I just wanted Bailey to like and trust me. And now he's sick because of me!" His pacing picked up in intensity.

April understood his feelings, having once overfed her dog, resulting in it becoming sick and leading to an expensive vet bill, which her father made her pay off. "OK, so, you know it now. What's important is that we do what we can to make sure Bailey gets better."

"We?"

"Well, since I didn't explain the whole oats thing properly, I'm somewhat to blame here. So let's get a game plan together."

They quickly put in place a schedule involving walking Bailey around the coral slowly 4 times an hour. At the pace they chose, it took 5-6 minutes for each walking session, leaving around 10 minutes for resting between each walk. At first, Bailey resisted. But as late afternoon wore into evening, he was more receptive to the exercise.

"We better get something to eat," April said as she looked at her watch. "They'll be closing the mess hall soon."

Jessie hadn't thought about the fact that dinner time had approached and was just about over as he concentrated on keeping Bailey on a regular schedule. "You go ahead. I want to stay here and make sure he doesn't lie down. I wanna keep him walking, like the doc said."

April felt guilty for leaving the two of them but she hadn't eaten anything all day. "I'll be back soon." She bounded off for the mess hall as Jessie started another walking session with Bailey.

"I'm really sorry buddy," he said as they walked around the perimeter of the coral. "I never meant to hurt you. Ya gotta know that." He hoped if Bailey didn't understand his words, he at least understood his tone and the sincerity behind it, like April had told him. "You're the closest thing I've had to a pet and I managed to screw it up. Just like I've screwed up everything lately. You probably have never known anyone that took proper care of you and then I came along and proved to be just as bad as everyone else. But I didn't mean to hurt you and I promise I'm gonna do better by you. I want you to know what it's like to have someone that cares about you like my dad cared about me. I can at least do that for you."

After the walk was finished, Jessie led Bailey to his stall to rest, then went to refresh the water bucket. When he returned, Bailey took a long drink, which Jessie took as a good sign. But he could see the horse's side was still bloated.

With the chilly night air settling in, he grabbed a horse blanket to cover Bailey but was concerned the weight of it might actually add to the horse's discomfort. So instead, he ran to his room and got the extra blanket that had been sitting on the foot of his bed. He draped it over Bailey's back, pleased it was big enough to cover his entire body from the neck base to the tail.

Shortly after the next walking session, April returned and handed Jessie a sandwich. "Didn't want you to starve."

Jessie was grateful for the food but too worried to eat.

"There's no need for you to punish yourself," April chided. "You can spare a few minutes to eat it. Besides, what are you gonna do when it's time for 'lights out'? You're gonna have to leave Bailey at some point."

He shook his head violently. "No way! I'm not leaving him tonight, not until I can see he's feeling better."

"So you're gonna stay up all night, walking him around the corral?" She thought the idea was a little extreme.

"If that's what it takes."

The determination in Jessie's voice informed April that she was not about to win any argument that included a suggestion for him to get some sleep. "Well, if you're staying up all night, I am too. I'll go and get us some blankets."

***

"You've never asked me why I'm here," Jessie stated after April and he started walking Bailey for the uncounted time that day. "I mean, it's obvious why I'm here. I'm a total screw-up. But you've never asked me for the details of *how* I screwed up."

"Just because you're here doesn't mean you're a total screw-up. It just means you've made some mistakes. And the details don't matter to me. Unless you murdered somebody, of course. I guess it would be good if I knew that. Especially if it was a dark, cold night and you did the dastardly deed in a stable or some such place."

"I'm not that bad," he replied with a smile. Her humor was one of the many things Jessie liked about April. She seemed sincere and caring, and it helped that he thought she was hot! His smile quickly went south however. "But I guess I'm bad enough. I definitely don't want to be. I've just got a lot of stuff I'm dealing with."

"So you tell me the details if you want or you don't. Either way, it's not going to change my opinion of you."

"I'm not sure I want to know your opinion of me but I'm going to ask anyway." He braced himself, hoping she didn't have too accurate a sense of what he was like.

She paused and looked at him for a moment, causing Jessie to feel even more apprehensive. "Believe it or not, I think you're pretty cool. You obviously care about animals, which already ranks you high with me. I think you must have a sense about them because you got Bailey to warm up to you pretty quickly and you are taking great care of him now so that tells me a lot about you. If an animal, with all of their natural intuition that we can't even comprehend, trusts you, I believe I can too…even if you did almost kill him."

Even though he knew she was just giving him a good-natured ribbing, there was some truth in her statement.

"You probably don't realize it but it's very likely you saved Bailey's life tonight," April said reassuringly. "No one else had noticed there was anything wrong with him!"

"Yeah, looks like I finally did something right in my life."

"I have a feeling you've done a whole lot more than this one thing right in your life." She didn't like that he was so down on himself. "Like it sounds as if you had a real good relationship with your dad, which I think is awesome. Wish I had that."

"He was great." Jessie stared at the ground as they walked. "I miss him a lot."

She could hear the sadness in his voice whenever Jessie spoke about his dad. She was envious of the emotion he clearly felt about his father. "Anyway, in answer to your original question, I have a strong sense that you're a good person who's made a few mistakes. Who hasn't? Mistakes don't make you bad."

"I really didn't mean to do the stuff I've done."

April shook her head. "That sounds a bit phony, don't you think? I mean, you may not have planned to do the things that landed you here, but you did them. At any point prior to doing whatever, you could have told yourself not to…but you didn't. I'm pretty sure you know right from wrong so if you're going to say you didn't mean to do the things you did, you had the opportunity to *not* do them and you chose the opposite. So, like I said, your statement sounds a bit phony to me."

Her brutal honesty was jarring for Jessie. But he knew she was essentially correct. He had felt guilt for what he was *about* to do several times. But each time he went through with it and each time he got caught. Maybe he wanted to get caught. His mind was still trying to sort all that out.

When they were finished with Bailey's walk, Jessie grabbed a brush, hoping the soothing feeling of being brushed would help the animal. Bailey inched closer to Jessie as the brush made long strokes down his neck, which Jessie took as a good sign. After Bailey was sufficiently groomed, Jessie filled the water bucket with fresh water, even though the water in it was only a few minutes old. He wanted to be sure he did as much as he could to relieve Bailey's discomfort.

Jessie looked at his watch, then over at a dead-tired looking April. *Why wouldn't she be?* It was 2:00 in the morning! "You better get to bed. You look beat."

"I think I'll hang out with your two for a while, just to make sure you don't forget to do something, like refill the water bucket for the thousandth time." April flashed him an admiring smile.

"I'm not forgetting anything tonight. Everything the doc told me to do is getting done. You get some sleep. We'll be OK."

April didn't make any type of gesture that would indicate she was thinking of leaving so it looked to Jessie like the three of them were going to be together through the night, or until Bailey showed signs of some sort of relief.

They continued talking as the night wore on, with April learning more about Jesse's relationship with his father, which she found impressive. But she thought it odd that he didn't talked about his mother the entire night, except to say that he was certain she didn't understand anything about him or what he was going through.

She also learned of his love for animals, which made sense considering what they were doing through the night.

She even learned that he had never kissed a girl.

And Jessie learned more about April. Her love of animals seemed to match his, which made sense considering the connection he felt with her from the first time they met.

But the description she offered of her home life made it sound as if it was anything but ideal.

"So what's the deal with your parents?" Jessie asked.

April had never talked about her home life with anyone who wasn't already familiar with it. But on that particular night, she felt as though she had found someone from outside her world whom she could confide in. "Let's just say my dad and I don't have a great relationship."

"Why not?"

"Basically because he's not a nice guy." She was tentative with what she shared. She didn't want to scare him off.

"What about your mom?"

"She left when I was young. Apparently my grandmother did the same thing. It appears that women in my family can't seem to stay with their men. I definitely understand how my mom couldn't stay with my dad."

The noticeable sadness in her voice put Jessie on edge. "Does he hit you?"

"No, no, nothing like that," she was quick to respond. "But he beats me down with his words. It's mentally exhausting being around him. He's miserable all the time and he likes making others feel the same."

Jessie wasn't sure how to respond. He knew he was lucky to have the relationship he had had with his dad. Most of his friends weren't nearly as close to either of their parents. But he had never met someone who had a father who abused them, either physically or mentally.

"My uncle helps me as much as he can. But even he doesn't like to be around his brother. They get into some heated arguments about how my dad acts, which means his visits never last very long. So my home life is the reason I'm here."

Jessie wanted to know more but instinctively felt as though he shouldn't push. April's demeanor was easy to read, even for someone as inexperienced with women as he was.

As a new day started to creep over the horizon, it was time to start another walk around the corral. They prepared to start the routine, leading Bailey out of the barn. Suddenly the animal stopped dead in his tracks. No matter what Jessie or April did, he wouldn't budge. Out of a bad habit, Jessie almost grabbed some oats to entice Bailey but caught himself before he even moved towards the oat bag.

After several moments, Bailey's tail rose up and he let loose the loudest and longest fart imaginable. Jessie and April immediately broke into hysterical laughter as Bailey proceeded to let loose something else of a more solid nature. The two of them stared at the steaming pile at their feet as they frantically waved the smell away from their noses.

"Whoa, that's nasty," Jessie exclaimed.

As they both moved away from the source of the intense odor invading their nostrils, April motioned towards Bailey, who had started running on his own. "But it seems as though our patient is feeling a whole lot better!"

They smiled in relief as they watched Bailey run around the corral several times, building up speed as he obviously continued to feel better with each passing minute. His smooth movement was mesmerizing to Jessie. He had never seen such a large animal move so gracefully. He wished he could move through his life as smoothly. And he wished the same for April. He admired the fact that she seemed well-adjusted to her less-than-ideal life. He needed to do the same.

Chapter Eleven

Kelsie had been looking forward to Saturday ever since her conversation with Brice. And as she drove to the facility, she realized she was also apprehensive. She didn't want to risk upsetting Jessie but she really did want to see him.

Brice had called to tell her about her son's harrowing night with Bailey. Even though she knew Jessie wasn't allowed to make phone calls, Kelsie wished he had called her himself to tell her the details. She was having a hard time remembering the last time he had called to her tell her about anything that had happened in his life.

As she approached the gate at Redemption, her worry about how Jessie would react to her being there intensified. With him being so interested in telling her about Bailey during the two minute phone call Brice allowed him to make, she hadn't been able to ask him if he minded her coming to visit. She hoped Brice had told him she was coming.

It doesn't matter she told herself. *I need to see my son.*

As she drove up the long driveway, the area was buzzing with the usual activity she witnessed every time she had been there but she noticed something different was happening this time. In the middle of the field just beyond the corral, a large pile of wood was being stacked and a circle of landscaping rocks was being laid around it. *Wonder what's going on there?* she thought to herself.

She parked her car and started towards the corral as a cold breeze came up over the field. While no snow had fallen yet, the cold temperature made her feel certain that the first snowfall of the season would soon arrive. She pulled the collar up on her heavy winter coat.

As Kelsie approached the corral, Brice emerged from the stables and made a beeline for her. "Hey there", she called out as she waved to him.

"Hey there yourself", he replied. "Glad you could make it." The smile on his face gave her a pretty solid understanding of exactly how he was feeling.

Kelsie matched his broad smile. "Of course I made it. I want to see Jessie. I miss him."

"Is he the only one you want to see?" Brice asked with a semi-hurt tone but with hope in his eyes.

"Well, of course I want to meet Bailey too!" She rolled her eyes in mock ridicule.

They both laughed as the affectionate stare between them lingered a bit longer than might be considered usual.

Kelsie started towards the stable with Brice by her side. She was surprised to see Jessie confidently riding a beautiful horse she assumed to be Bailey. It didn't go unnoticed by her that he seemed to be talking and riding with a young lady about whom Kelsie knew nothing. Knowing of her son's inexperience with the opposite sex, she hoped it wasn't a bad thing.

Jessie saw his mother approaching and gave her a quick wave. Ever since Brice had told him she was coming, he hadn't been certain of how he felt about it.

As Brice and Kelsie arrived within earshot of Jessie, he was the first to speak. "Hey Mom."

Kelsie waved as Jessie approached with the young lady close behind. "Hi honey."

Jessie immediately turned beet-red at how his mother addressed him in front of Brice and April. Kelsie could see his discomfort and immediately tried to mask it.

"So is this the infamous Bailey whom I heard kept you up all night?" As Bailey got close enough, Kelsie reached out to scratch his nose.

"In the flesh," Jessie beamed, happy to have the center of conversation be anything but himself.

"He seems to be doing well now," Kelsie observed.

"Yeah, he's a whole lot better," Jessie proclaimed, looking over at April. "We made sure of it."

April held her hands up in surrender. "Hey, it was your idea to stay up all night and walk him every 15 minutes like clockwork. You did all the work. I just kept you company."

Kelsie looked at April as she extended her hand. "I don't believe we've met. I'm Kelsie."

"April, this is my Mom," Jessie stated matter-of-factly.

"It's nice to meet you," Kelsie stated with a genuine smile as they shook hands. "Thanks for helping Jessie out with Bailey."

"Like I said, he did all the work. But I was happy to keep them both company," April replied, hoping Kelsie didn't think anything else was going on, since it wasn't.

Kelsie continued to pet Bailey, admiring the horse's sturdy stance. It had been years since she had been so close to a horse. "You look impressive on him Jessie."

Jessie blushed again. He always felt embarrassed whenever she complimented him on something in front of others but realized he didn't know why. However, he knew that he looked anything but impressive sitting on Bailey's back. He was surprised he was able to stay in the saddle!

"Oh, stop blushing," she teased him. She really was impressed at how he rode, especially considering he had never been on a horse until he came to Redemption.

Like mother; like son she thought.

Brice suddenly had an idea. "How about we all go for a ride together?"

Before Kelsie could voice her approval, Jessie spoke up. "Mom doesn't know how to ride, Brice."

"Shows how much you know," Brice corrected him. "Your mom is a very good rider as I recall. Unless she's lost her touch." He flashed Kelsie a sly smile.

Jessie looked at his mother with surprise in his eyes. "Mom?"

"I did have a life before you came along, you know." She smiled at her son. "And even though it's been a while, I'm pretty sure I still know how to stay in the saddle."

"Great," Brice proclaimed, his enthusiasm for the adventure palpable.

He immediately spotted two kids who were heading towards the stables and waved them over. "If you two are done, I'll take them off your hands and take care of them when we are done riding."

Walking over to the horse Brice was holding in place, Kelsie felt butterflies in her stomach. She thought it was entirely possible she had shrunk since she had last mounted a horse as the beautiful one she was approaching seemed to tower over her. It had been years since she had mounted a horse and was thankful when Brice offered to help her up. Her instincts kicked in as she held onto the saddle properly and settled into it. The lessons she had learned so long ago came rushing back as she sat high off the ground, her previous nervousness quickly replaced by anticipation. She was no longer worried about embarrassing herself. She was ready to hit the meadow at full gallop!

"You feel OK up there?" Brice asked, before he dared let go of the reins.

"Like I never dismounted," she stated in a voice that left no doubt of her full confidence.

Brice smiled and handed her the reins, then mounted his own horse. "April, you have any particular destination in mind?"

She looked at Jessie with a smile. "I think the waterfall is a good one."

"What's that?" Jessie queried.

"Only the most beautiful place on the ranch," Brice offered.

"It's a little bit of a ride but it's worth it." April winked at Jessie as she started off across the meadow at easy gallop so that no one would feel obligated to try and keep up with her. Brice and Kelsie quickly joined in as Jessie watched his mother in astonishment while she expertly rode across the field. Before it was too late, he realized he was being left in the dust and made haste to join the others.

Before long, Kelsie was out in front of the group riding at an impressive gate for someone who hadn't been on a horse in years. But once she felt the gentle nature of the animal beneath her, she instinctively knew she was going to be fine and became anxious to stretch its legs. Soon Brice caught up to her while April and Jessie were enjoying a more leisurely pace.

For Kelsie, being on a horse again took her back to her childhood, away from haunting memories and away from the legal troubles her son was encountering. She smiled as she realized she felt free of it all. She wished it was a feeling that could last forever. She looked over at Brice and found herself wondering what it would be like for her today if things had been different during their years in school.

What if he hadn't been the 'bad boy' in school? she asked herself.

Then she contemplated…*what if I hadn't been so worried about always doing the right thing back then?*

A realization popped into her head. *If any of that had been the case, you wouldn't have Jessie and you wouldn't have known the pleasures of a good, strong marriage.* She felt a bit ashamed of what she had been thinking. Even with everything she and Jessie were going through, she was grateful for the life she had. She believed there was a reason for everything.

April took the lead as they slowed their pace and approached the edge of a wooded area. They followed her slowly along a well-worn path and after about 5 minutes, Kelsie could hear the sound of water. Before long, they came upon a pool of crystal clear spring water at the base of what she estimated to be a 30 foot waterfall. But this wasn't a typical waterfall that fell straight down from a tall edge. This one fell gently down a steep slope, twisting its way through rocks of various sizes, all worn smooth by years of water flowing over them. Ferns and trees sprouted out over the water as it trickled its way down to the pool, the last of the fall colors adding to the beauty of the scene while the sun dancing off the moving water made it sparkle. Kelsie stared at the shimmering sight for several moments, fully appreciating its beauty. Then she closed her eyes and listened to the music of the water. It was the most relaxing sound she had heard in a long while, disturbed only by the sound of amazement coming from Jessie.

"Wow, this place is cool!" he exclaimed. "It's just like a place I went camping once."

Kelsie knew exactly the trip he was talking about. It was one of many Jessie had taken with his father and they both had talked about it for weeks afterwards. She watched Jessie closely, wondering if the memory would make him sad. Brice watched too, to see what the memory might trigger. But Jessie just kept looking at the water as it made its way down the slope, smiling all the while. Kelsie wondered if it was a good sign but realized the professional in the group was the only one that would know the answer. She also knew she couldn't ask. So she decided to simply enjoy watching her son enjoy the same beauty she was seeing.

But the professional in the group actually didn't have the answer to her question. He simply tucked the observation away in his memory in case it might help later.

"This place must be especially beautiful with snow on the ground," Kelsie mused to no one in particular.

"Spectacular is the word I would use," Brice confirmed. "Come here a month from now and you'll see." He looked at Kelsie as she met his glance and winked.

She was about to agree to his suggestion but reality came flooding back to her, reminding her she couldn't make even the simplest plans at that moment. Brice wasn't sure what to make of her serious expression as she turned back to the waterfall. He was thankful to see her relax a bit after staring at the waterfall again for a few moments.

"Let's give the horses a chance to drink while we stretch our legs," April suggested.

They all dismounted and led their horses to the edge of the pond to quench their thirst while they explored the area. Naturally, Jessie and April paired off, each pretending to be interested in the various rocks surrounding the water but clearly staying near each other so they could talk in hushed tones dotted with periodic laughter.

Kelsie looked at the two young people as she spoke to Brice. "Something going on there I should know about?"

"Hard to say. Seems pretty clear they are interested in each other."

"Do you think that's a good thing? I hear plenty of horror stories about relationships that start in rehab."

Brice's disapproving glare made her quickly rephrase her statement.

"Sorry, I know this isn't rehab. But is it a good idea for something to start under these circumstances? Two people going thru difficulties doesn't seem like the best circumstance to start a relationship that could go on forever."

"Do you always go from zero to sixty?" There was genuine disbelief in his tone. "They are just getting to know each other. Who said anything about 'a relationship'? Did your first relationship last forever?"

Kelsie paused for several moments. "No." She turned to stare into the woods. "It ended about 18 months ago."

It took a few beats for Brice to comprehend what she was telling him. He felt foolish for his statement as he realized her first relationship would still be ongoing if things had turned out the way Kelsie planned.

"Sorry." He let his one-word apology hang between them for a few moments. "But let's not assume anything about Jessie and April right now. I think it's a good sign he is opening up to her. I'm having a hard time cracking that nut so him opening up to anyone is a good thing. Let's just accept that for what it is."

Kelsie looked at Jessie and April as they laughed at something one of them had said. With the backdrop of the waterfall and the sun shining down on all of them that beautiful afternoon, she would have been happy to have the moment last a lifetime. But she was satisfied for it to last for as long as the afternoon would allow.

The four of them spent the rest of the afternoon walking in pairs, Kelsie and Brice admiring the beauty of the setting without discussing much about their respective pasts while April and Jessie talked about the future, which Jessie was hesitant to do since his immediate future would have a very definitive effect on his extended future and he didn't feel very optimistic. April encouraged him to think positively but it wasn't easy for him to do.

No mention was made of a future between any of them. Kelsie needed to get through Christmas before she could figure out where her life was headed. And Jessie simply couldn't think that far ahead. But April could. And so could Brice

When the sun started to dip in the sky as dusk approached, they reluctantly mounted their horses and headed back to the facility.

Back to reality.

It was too soon for Jessie.

Kelsie too.

Chapter Twelve

"I found him! I found him!" Tina's voice came shouting through Kelsie's phone before she could offer a greeting. Her excitement was evident, although Kelsie had no idea what she was talking about.

"You wanna give me a little context to this proclamation?" she asked of her friend.

Tina took an audibly deep breath and attempted to control her excitement before continuing. "Remember the guy you said was giving me the 'once-over' at the coffee shop a couple weeks ago?"

"How could I forget? You looked like a Cheshire-cat after bumping into him."

"Oh, I did not," Tina rebutted, although she knew it was very likely that Kelsie's statement was completely accurate.

"OK, you tell yourself that. But in the meantime, I'm assuming that's the guy you found?"

"Yes! I ran into him again at the place I usually go to for lunch. I was in line waiting to order and he spotted me. He was so cute when he came over to say "Hi". He was afraid I wouldn't remember him."

"He obviously didn't comprehend the initial impression he made!"

"I know, like I was going to forget those eyes anytime soon!"

"But how do you know he didn't think you'd remember him?"

"He told me later how nervous he was to come over and talk to me."

"Later?" Kelsie was starting to worry that her friend had done something very unlike her.

"He asked me if I'd have lunch with him. I was hesitant to do it but I'm glad I did. He's so nice and funny and smart."

"And don't forget good-looking," Kelsie could easily finish her friend's thought, which was currently zeroed in on this relative stranger.

Tina sighed. "That fact does not hurt the situation at all."

"So how come you haven't seen him again before now? Don't you eat at the same place almost every day?"

"Normally..yes. But I've been so busy lately I haven't had time to go out so I've been having something brought into the office. But today I just needed to take a break from my desk. And there he was!"

"Hoping you would stroll into his life one day."

"Something like that. He transferred here last month from Texas and works at the law firm in the building next to the one I'm in. He has lunch at the same place every day because he doesn't really know his way around yet and he said it was the first place he found that had a decent BBQ sauce. Apparently they take their sauce seriously in Texas."

"Sounds believable. I'm glad you ran into him again."

"So am I because he's asked me to dinner Saturday."

"Congratulations!" Kelsie was genuinely happy for her friend, who hadn't dated anyone for quite a while. "I'll expect a full report Sunday morning. Unless, of course, you are otherwise occupied," she teased.

"Oh I'd love to say I will be too busy to give you the details but a first date is way too soon. You know me better than that!"

"I do. And I'm thankful you're not planning to change your ways now."

"It'll be tough but I can hold out," Tina sounded slightly unsure of her resolve in the matter. "Although I'm not really sure for how long."

"Remember our motto...'First date is a hug, second date is a kiss, third date...let whatever happens...happen!" They both giggled. "But seriously, I'm happy for you." Kelsie continued. "I hope he turns out to be a genuinely nice guy. You deserve that."

"Thanks. I can't wait. I'm sure I'll talk your ear off about it afterwards but for now I'll let you get back to work."

"OK, call if you need any wardrobe advice."

"Will do." Tina was about to end the call. "Oh, I almost forgot. How's Jessie? You went to see him yesterday, right?"

"He's doing good, thanks. Still not *there* yet but he is actually show-ing interest in a girl he met there. Brice seems to think it's a good thing. I'm not sure though."

"Did you meet her?"

"Yes. She seems very nice and pleasant. But I don't think the setting is actually very conducive for starting a relationship. And I don't know that Jessie showing interest in someone who is also a troubled-teen is really a smart move at this point."

"You worry too much. Love can be found just about anywhere. School, a counseling program, even, possibly, in a lunch spot." Tina's smile could almost be heard through the phone.

"Let's not use the "L" word just yet, for either of you."

Kelsie's slightly stern tone told Tina her friend was right. She needed to get the first date out of the way before even thinking about anything beyond it.

Tina sighed at the thought of her pending date. "You're right, of course. You always were the sensible one. Anyway, gotta run. I'll call you tomorrow."

Kelsie smiled as she put down her phone. It could be entirely pos-sible that things were looking up for everyone in her life. She could only hope!

***

It was time for another session and oddly enough, Jessie wasn't dreading it. He awoke refreshed after spending the previous day rid-ing, exploring and feeling...normal. It was almost like he and his dad were on one of their adventures again. So for almost a whole day, Jessie's world didn't feel like it was imploding. It was only when he went to bed and reflected on the day's events that the feeling of loss started to creep back into his thoughts. He tried to not let that feeling diminish his memories of the day though. It had been a good one!

Standing in the breakfast line, Jessie realized that, other than Max, the only person he had met during his time at Redemption whom he would consider a friend was April. And she was never at breakfast. He only seemed to run into her at the stables or around the ranch long after breakfast. And that morning, he felt like eating breakfast with someone. With his tray loaded down with cereal, toast and a bowl of fresh fruit, he surveyed the mess hall, spotting Max sitting by himself. He made his way over to his roommate.

"Want some company?"

Max responded without looking up from the food he was picking at on his tray. "Do you think this qualifies as food?" He had chosen the scrambled eggs that morning, which to Jessie did have a resemblance to rubber.

"That's why you should always go for the cereal. You know exactly what you're going to get." He sat down on the opposite side of the table.

"Very wise," Max stated as he pushed the tray away and grabbed the banana from Jessie's tray. "Mind?"

"Go for it. I've got plenty here."

Max peeled the banana as he looked at Jessie. He would be attracted to him if he was gay. But Max knew Jessie wasn't and appreciated the fact that he had befriended him anyway. Making friends hadn't always been easy for Max. The only other friend he had made while at Redemption had already done his time. But Max smiled at the thought of hopefully seeing him again soon.

Jessie dug into his bowl of cereal with gusto. "What are you up to today?"

Max responded with just a hint of secretive, dramatic flair. "Word is there is going to be some sort of festivities here that will include a bonfire this Saturday. I'm gonna see what I can do to help set it up."

"Look at you getting involved." Jessie winked.

"Beats sitting around waiting for more counseling." Max was there only because his parents refused to accept him as he was, which led to outbursts that a judge, with no knowledge or apparent concern about his situation, decided could potentially bring harm to someone. So he had been sent to Redemption to "work on his anger issues". But he looked at it as a vacation from the source of his issues. He was basically using his time there to figure out how to best keep the peace until he could live on his own and be himself without having to explain everything he did to his parents. "What's on your agenda?"

"More counseling," Jessie said with a smile. Max rolled his eyes. "But then I'll spend the rest of the day with Bailey."

"You really like that horse," Max acknowledged, slightly jealous he didn't have something to hold his own interests.

"He's great. And now that's he's better, I want to make sure he doesn't get sick again. Besides, he listens to whatever I want to tell him without passing judgment. And, he doesn't steal my bananas!" Jessie threw a waded up napkin at his breakfast companion.

Max bounced off his chair in a mock fit of rage. "I'm being attacked!! I must run for my life!"

Jessie laughed as he watched Max making his exit, in search of the person in charge of the upcoming festivities. He liked Max but wondered if they would be friends outside of their current surroundings. He figured he could use some new friends and decided to do his best to make that happen as soon as he was able.

After depositing his tray and empty dishes in their proper place, Jessie made his way towards Brice's office. He looked out the big picture window as he passed through the main room and saw storm clouds gathering. He wouldn't mind seeing some snow falling. It had been a mild fall, which was great for his ride the previous day but he always liked it when there was snow on the ground for Christmas.

Christmas! He hadn't given any thought to the fact that the holiday was fast approaching. He certainly wasn't going to be doing his usual pre-holiday activities this year. *And whose fault is that?* he chided himself as he walked down the hall towards his morning appointment..

Brice looked up from his desk when he heard a knock on his open office door to find Jessie standing in the doorway. He looked at the clock on the wall. "You're early!"

Jessie knew he was but he wanted to get started. "Good morning to you too," he said with a bit of sarcasm in his voice and a smile on his face.

Brice laughed. "Seems you threw my morning off so much that I forgot my manners. Good morning."

Jessie smiled. "Figured I'd get an early start to the day. But if you need me to come back, I can." He was sincere but hoped that Brice was willing to start their session early.

"No problem," Brice assured him. "Go ahead and have seat. I'm almost finished."

Jessie took a seat in the chair directly across the desk from Brice and waited. He glanced out the window at the gathering clouds and hoped it wasn't a metaphor for the day/week ahead of him.

Brice put his pen down and switched from 'admin' to 'concerned listener' mode. He sat back in his chair, not making a move to come around and sit nearer to Jessie. "I've been meaning to congratulate you on helping Bailey through his difficulties. You did a great job with him."

"I didn't really do much."

"You did more than you think. You kept him moving, which relieved his discomfort. If left alone, he would have simply laid down and stayed there, which would have detrimental."

"I just did what the vet said."

"You did more than that. You showed Bailey that you cared about him, and that you wanted to help him. Your actions communicated a lot to him, something people don't seem to understand about animals. They're very intuitive."

Jessie hadn't previously considered what Brice was telling him but he hoped it was true. He liked the thought of Bailey understanding he was concerned and trying to help.

"So you stuck with him through the ordeal and saw things through to a good end. That's important."

"He's a cool horse. I didn't want to let him down."

Brice saw a glimmer of hope in Jessie's statement. He seemed a bit calmer, hopefully due to his part in the final outcome of Bailey's situation. "Do you have animals at home?"

"I always wanted a dog but we couldn't have one. My dad was allergic to them."

"Did that upset you, that you couldn't have a pet because of your father?"

Jessie considered the question, having never previously given it much thought. "No, I guess I understood," he shrugged. "It really wasn't a big deal."

"That's mature of you, to understand your father's comfort was more important than your desire to have a dog."

"Dad was pretty cool too."

"It's great that you two were close."

"Yeah, we did a lot of fun stuff together. He always had time for me, even when he was sick."

"What are some of the things you two would do?"

"He'd help me with my homework, taught me about baseball, stuff like that. We used to take a trip every summer, just the two of us. One year we went fishing; one year we camped. We'd go hiking and skiing together, lots of fun stuff.

"Sounds like you two had a lot of fun together."

Jessie smiled at the memories flooding his head. "He taught me a lot of stuff while we were having fun too."

"Like what?"

"When we went hiking for the first time, he could see I was getting worried about what we would do if we got lost. So he taught me how to navigate without a compass so I'd never have to worry about getting lost in the woods."

"That's a good thing to know. Wish my dad had taught me things like that." Brice enjoyed hearing details of the things Jessie did with his father. And he was sincere when he stated he wished his father had taught him...anything. "Off the top of your head, tell me a favorite memory of something your father did with you."

Jessie thought for several moments as he realized he had many moments to choose from. "One time, mom had to work late so dad had to handle dinner. Usually he'd order something from our favorite Italian place but that night he made pancakes for dinner. Mom would have had a fit if she knew. She always said we had to have at least two vegetables with whatever she made along with a salad. She says a balanced diet is important."

"She's right, of course," Brice said with a wink.

"That's why dad made blueberry pancakes! He figured she wouldn't get too mad if dinner involved fruit."

It was clear to Brice their conversation was allowing Jessie to fully appreciate the memory of a better time in his life.

"We laughed a lot while he made them. He burned the first couple so we had the windows open until mom got home to make sure she didn't smell anything, hoping dad wouldn't have to admit what he made for dinner."

"You probably don't realize this but you're smiling," Brice said as he smiled himself.

"Guess I am," Jessie reflected. "I haven't thought about that night in a while but it was a lot of fun. And delicious!"

"Glad I could help you to recall a good time," Brice responded. "From everything you've told me, it sounds your dad was pretty great."

"The best," Jessie quickly confirmed.

Brice watched intently, seeing a mixture of sadness and happiness in Jessie's eyes. "You miss him a lot, don't you?"

Jessie suddenly got quiet and the enthusiasm he had exuded moments earlier left him completely.

"Of course you do. He was an important part of your life and I'm sure you're feeling like nothing can take the place of everything he meant to you."

Jessie remained quiet.

"So it's important to remember the good times with your father as much as possible. It'll help to lessen the pain of losing him since being sad all the time isn't helping your situation. And I'm certain sadness is not what your father wanted you to feel all the time either."

"But I can't help it." Jessie looked out the window again, wishing he could wipe away the hole in his heart from where his sadness emanated.

"I think you can…if you try," Brice pressed. "I'm not saying it'll be easy but if you can dwell more on the good, fun memories of your father, think about things he taught you and remember that he wanted to best for you, you might find the sadness lessens just a bit each day. It's not fair that the time you had together as a family was cut short. But don't let that erase your memories of him. Hang onto those memories when you are feeling low and they'll help you through the tough moments that lie ahead."

Jessie stared at the floor without speaking.

Brice decided it was time to change the subject…slightly. "It's also important to remember there are still a lot of positive aspects to your life."

The look Jessie shot at Brice conveyed his annoyance at the statement.

"For instance, your mom seems pretty great too. It's obvious she cares about you a lot."

"It's not the same."

"No, but it can still be good. She can show you things too. And you can do fun things with her as well. She's already shown you that she can ride a horse. I'll bet she knows how to do other things that you would like too, things you might not have a clue she can do."

"I suppose," Jessie replied unconvinced. "Still not the same."

"Sometimes things have to change. And while the reason they changed for you isn't good, it doesn't mean that good can't come out of it. You live in a nice house?"

Jessie nodded.

"Do you feel like you need something your mother doesn't provide?"

"'Course not. She works hard and does a lot for me."

"So you have whatever you need?"

Jessie nodded.

"Computer, phone, games, food, clothes."

Jessie nodded.

"And I know you felt like you could talk to your dad about anything that was going on with you, no matter what it was."

"Yeah, he didn't judge me. He just helped me figure things out."

"So it's obvious you had a great relationship with your dad. And you probably realize that's pretty rare these days. Most kids aren't as lucky as you. Most would say you won the 'dad lottery'."

"Yeah, I don't know anyone else who can talk to their dad the way I did."

"So I want you to take a moment and think about this next question I'm going to ask, then give me your honest answer." Brice paused, wanting Jessie to concentrate on his inquiry. "Do you think you could talk to your mother in the same way?"

Jessie had never considered the question Brice posed. He had always talked to his dad about everything and never had to think about going to his mother regarding something that might be troubling him or that he needed to know. But Brice's simple question was not so simple to answer. Or was it? After thinking about it for several moments, the answer was as simple and clear as the single word he uttered.

"Yes."

Finally Brice thought to himself. *Maybe I'm getting somewhere.*

"So why do you think you've been acting out since your father died?"

Jessie had no answer. Or didn't want to have an answer.

"I'm thinking it has something to do with you wanting attention. Attention like your dad used to give you. But instead of getting the positive attention he provided, your actions are providing you with negative attention, which in turn is making you act out more. But you need to realize that the positive attention you have been seeking is available to you from your mother. Now is the time for her to be the positive influence in your life. But instead of letting her in, you seem to have shut her out. I'm pretty certain she can provide you more attention than most kids get these days. Do you think that's a fair assessment?"

Jessie stared at a bowl sitting on Brice's desk. It was just a simple bowl with no real distinct features. But it was easier to stare at the bowl than it was to honestly answer the question Brice posed.

"Look, you know that nothing can or ever will take the place of your father. But you also know that you have everything you need to grow up and be a strong and productive person. The person he was helping you to be. The sad truth is that you simply don't have your father here with you, which I'm certain you want more than anything. But no amount of pushing others for attention is going to bring him back. All it does in the end is make things tougher on your mom. So you need to figure out a way forward from your sadness, away from things that will only make your life worse in the end."

"And how exactly am I supposed to do that without him? He is the one who would help me figure things out." Despair was evident in Jessie's tone.

"Well, that's the one thing you haven't considered. You don't have to do it without him because he'll always be with you. The things that he taught you will resonate throughout your life, as they should. The things you did together, the memories of the good times you had together, these are what will keep him with you throughout the rest of your life. Remembering all the positive aspects of having him as your father will carry you through the sadness and help you to move forward. Don't dwell on the negative; the loss. Think instead of the things you did and the things you know he wanted you to do; the things he wanted you to achieve. He wanted the best for you and for you to be the best you can be."

Brice paused to let his words sink in. He could see that Jessie was trying to understand everything he was being told but he had one final thought to articulate. "I'm pretty sure it's safe to say he would be disappointed in your actions lately. So it's important to remember that living your life the way you know your father would want you to, and not taking for granted the positive things you have in your life, is the best way you can honor him. Which will, in turn, keep you on a more positive path. I hope this makes sense."

Brice studied Jessie as he sat quietly, hoping a realization might be taking shape within the young man. It could be the breakthrough that everyone who came through Redemption had to make. Usually tears of realization signified the metamorphosis was starting.

But there were no tears welling up in Jessie's eyes. No trembling. No quivering lip. Still, Brice could see that something was churning over and over in his head. It just may not be ready to come to the surface yet.

Brice had let his words hang in the air long enough. If something significant was going to happen, it would have happened. *Time to switch things up.* "Did you have fun yesterday?"

Jessie perked up a little as he responded with a firm nod.

"Me too."

"Still having a hard time processing that my mother knows how to ride a horse. I think I should have known that."

"Why would you if she hasn't ever ridden since you were born?"

"Guess I forget that my mom had a life before she met my dad."

"And believe it or not, she was your age at one time. So she probably had some things to work out at times too, just like you do. Just like all of us do."

Jessie's silence informed Brice he had given him enough to consider for one day, knowing that most people Jessie's age never considered their parents might have ever experienced similar issues to theirs. It was unnaturally common for teens to think that there was no way their parents could understand them, ever. Rather than make Jessie delve into those thoughts, Brice decided to let him consider them on his own.

"Before you go, I wanted to let you know we are having our annual pre-holiday bonfire this Saturday. It's always a lot of fun and we invite parents so if you want to invite your mom, you can give her a call. It's totally up to you." Which was true. It was a decision that was totally up to Jessie. But Brice was hoping to see Kelsie there.

***

Jessie entered his sleeping space and flopped onto the bed, his head spinning. He didn't seem to know his mother as well as he thought and it bothered him. Not knowing she could ride a horse was just one thing. *What else don't I know that I should?* he thought to himself. He churned thoughts over and over before realizing there was a simple solution to his dilemma. *It's not like she's gone and I can't find out more about her!* he thought. It was as simple as asking her about what she likes, what she used to do when she was his age and a thousand other things that he felt were important to know. His father shared so much with him. Now it was time to get the same from his mother. He wondered why he had never bothered to do it before.

In the meantime, he had a phone call to make. He walked to the office to seek out Anne, who apparently was the only person with access to the phone system at Redemption. She was a middle-aged woman who at first glance, due to the constant frown on her face, could easily be mistaken for a high school teacher who was always in a bad mood. But in reality, she was a sweetheart who took her job seriously yet always greeted anyone who addressed her with a smile.

"Hi Anne, I think Brice told you I was going to be coming by."

"Hi Jessie!" She beamed at him as he approached her desk. "Yes, Brice told me it was OK for you to use the phone." She pointed to a small table in the corner, next to a chair. "Just dial the number directly." She gave him a sly wink. "I'm sure your mother will be very happy to hear from you."

Jessie sat down next to the phone, thankful that its location gave him a bit of privacy. He dialed the number and waited.

Kelsie glanced at her phone and almost let it go to voice-mail, like she always did with numbers she didn't know. Then she realized it could be someone calling about Jessie. Her thoughts went quickly from *who is trying to sell me something* to *please let Jessie be OK!* She answered trying not to sound too anxious.

"Hello?" She held her breath.

"Hey Mom."

Kelsie exhaled audibly. "Jessie! Is everything OK? Where are you calling from?" she hoped he hadn't 'escaped'.

"Everything's cool Mom, don't panic." Jessie could picture her white as a sheet, worrying about why he was calling.

"I'm not panicking," she lied a little. "I'm just wondering why you're calling? Thought phone calls weren't allowed."

"They aren't. But Brice gave me special dispensation to give you a call."

"I hope not so you can tell me to come pick you up because they've given up." She wasn't sure the levity she was trying to convey would be perceived as it was intended.

"Brutal Mom." Jessie wasn't sure the levity he was trying to convey would be perceived as intended either.

"Just kidding."

He laughed. "Me too."

Kelsie was greatly relieved. "Glad they haven't dulled your sense of humor. So what's the special occasion? You save April's horse?"

"Nothing that exciting." He smiled at the thought of doing something for April. "Brice wanted me to let you know they're having a bonfire this Saturday. You can come if you want."

Kelsie was taken aback. "Oh!"

"Supposed to be fun. There's gonna be a band and stuff."

"What's the occasion?"

"Some sorta holiday thing they do every year."

"Sounds nice. Would you like me to come out for it?"

Jessie realized he hadn't fully considered how he would feel about her being at the bonfire. But he recalled being a little excited when Brice suggested he invite her so he figured inviting her was something he actually wanted to do.

"If you wanna come, I'm cool with it."

She realized that might be the closest thing she was going to get to an actual invitation. And as she thought about it, she realized it was possibly a good sign that maybe he was letting her penetrate the wall he had built around himself. *Could be a good chance for us to connect,* she thought. Plus, it sounded like it would be fun. She had yet to do anything fun for the holidays.

"Sounds like a great time!" Before he could change his mind, she added, "See you Saturday. Love you. Bye." She ended the call with no further comment.

But she was already looking forward to the bonfire.

Chapter Thirteen

When Kelsie arrived for the bonfire festivities just after dark, there were people milling around the grounds, dancing to music the DJ was spinning or just sitting and talking. A roaring bonfire was blazing in the middle of all the activity and people of all ages were gathered around, making s'mores or simply warming themselves on what had turned into a rather cold evening.

As she walked through the crowd looking for Jessie, she found herself lost in her thoughts, wondering how everyone at the gathering was connected. How many had been a part of the Redemption community at one time or another and come back for a visit? How many people there were parents of kids enrolled in the program? How many were friends checking on friends? Who had family there now or had family there in the past?

Just as she was about to turn her attention back to the seemingly impossible task of finding her son, Kelsie literally ran smack into a woman. "Oh, I'm so sorry! I'm not looking where I'm going. Are you OK?"

"No worries!" she replied. "I'm obviously not doing a great job of looking where I'm going either." She put her hand out to shake Kelsie's. "I'm Kim."

The full-figured woman was short with a pleasant face that was free of the worried look Kelsie seemed to have plastered on her face constantly during recent months. She couldn't imagine Kim had a child there, certain a worried look was standard-issue for anyone with a loved one at Redemption.

Kelsie introduced herself as they clasped hands.

"You trying to find your kid too?"

Kelsie grinned. "I have one here somewhere. Do you have..." She stopped herself from finishing the question, suddenly feeling awkward. She stared blankly at Kim.

"…a troubled kid in need of help?" Kim finished Kelsie's thought without a twinge of embarrassment. "It's OK to say it." She swept her hand around at the crowd. "Seems like we aren't alone."

Kelsie was struck by Kim's attitude. It was true, they weren't alone. But she seemed to be at ease with whatever situation she was dealing with. Kelsie wanted to feel the same, yet wasn't handling it nearly as well as her new acquaintance appeared to be. "No, we certainly aren't alone in this struggle, unfortunately."

Kim nodded. "But fortunately, there are places like this that can help us. And our loved ones."

"So you do have a child here?"

"Had. He graduated a little over a week ago. And the difference I see in him is like night and day!" Her smile said it all.

"I've been hoping to see a difference in mine but so far, not so much." She tried to plaster a smile on her face but couldn't muster anything that anyone with a brain couldn't see through.

"Believe me, you will." Kim knew exactly how Kelsie felt. Her youngest had been a tough nut to crack and his time at Redemption was not without drama. But her son had come through the experience truly changed so she knew there was hope. "They know what they're doing here. I have no idea what they said that got my son back on track but they did and that's all I need to know." She put her hand on Kelsie's shoulder. "Don't give up hope. Your kid will get through it and be better off for coming here, I'm certain of it. If they could help my son, they can help yours."

"You seem pretty confident in the counselors here." Kelsie hoped Kim's enthusiasm was not supplying her with false hope.

"Couldn't be more so! Our son was acting out in the most irrational ways. My husband and I simply couldn't get through to him or get him to see what he was doing was going to lead him straight to a life he didn't want for himself. I could tell he was scared about the consequences but he still did the most ridiculous things. This was our last resort. Thankfully, it all worked out in the end."

Kelsie smiled at Kim's story. "So if you don't mind me asking, why are you back if your son graduated? I hope he didn't slip up."

"Oh no, he's doing fantastic. But he asked if he could come tonight because he had heard this event is so much fun. From what I understand, a lot of former participants come back for it."

Kelsie was relieved. "That explains all the new faces. I was worried there had been an unusual influx of troubled youth!"

Kim smiled and nodded. "Yeah, most of the people here aren't current residents, thankfully."

"I had no idea they did anything like this until my son called and invited me." She let out a chuckle. "I could almost see his counselor watching him to make sure he actually dialed my number!"

Kim rolled her eyes and laughed. "Oh, yes, they can never appear to be so un-cool as to act like they want us around at any time."

Kelsie nodded in agreement. "And now I can't even find him so I can embarrass him."

"As any good mother should." Kim added with a broad smile, "as much as we possibly can!"

They both laughed as Kelsie realized she felt relaxed for the first time in a long while when talking about anything that involved Jessie. She was starting to wish the night could go on forever.

"It seems as though the rumors are indeed true," Kim stated as she looked around at the people enjoying themselves. "This is a fun event! However, I know the real reason my son wanted to be here is because he's got a bit of a crush on someone he met here. Pretty sure he really just wants them to spend some time together tonight."

"My son seems to be developing a relationship with someone he met here as well." Kelsie still wasn't sure how she felt about that. "Have you met her yet?"

"Him. Seems like a very nice kid. Glad my son has good taste in boyfriends."

Kelsie was impressed that this woman she had just met very matter-of-factly and quite naturally shared with her something about her son that some parents might share sheepishly...or not at all. She appreciated Kim's candor. "I'm thinking your son is lucky to have such a supportive mother."

Kim realized she hadn't ever had anyone accept what she just shared so easily and naturally as Kelsie did. Or say what Kelsie said. "Well, I'll admit that when he was born, this isn't exactly the scenario I envisioned. And I struggled with it when he told me…for about a minute. What it really comes down to for me is, as long as he's happy, healthy and safe, that's what's important. Everything else is just details that matter only as much as you let them."

"You are a refreshingly sensible voice amongst all the craziness these days."

"I call things the way I see them!"

Finally, Kim spotted Hunter and waved in his direction. "Oh, there's the sly devil. I better get to him while I can see him." She dug into her purse and handed Kelsie a card. "Here's my number. Give me a call if it seems like things are getting to be too much for you." She flashed a caring smile. "Sometimes it helps to talk to someone who has been there."

Kelsie accepted the card and greatly appreciated Kim's thoughtfulness. "There is a very good chance you'll be sorry you gave me this. I might just burn up your phone."

"No worries if you do. We mothers of troubled teens need to stick together!" She turned in the direction of where she had seen her son. "Give me a call, I mean it!" Then she dissolved into the crowd of dancers as the music continued pumping across the grounds.

Kelsie continued in her quest to find Jessie, Brice, April…someone she knew! As she weaved through the crowd, seeing so many faces she was certain were not currently program participants, she was glad that so many people appeared to have been helped by the program. It struck her as a good sign that many former attendees, like Kim's son, wanted to come back for the event. She hoped that one of the reasons they returned was to thank their counselors. Surrounded by so many people that had been helped at Redemption, she desperately hoped her son would be one of the facility's success stories.

Finally, she spotted April at the edge of the bonfire. Figuring Jessie would be with nearby, she started in her direction. As she got closer, she could see Jessie next to her as they roasted marshmallows, preparing to smash them between two layers of graham crackers with chocolate in-between. As she approached, both of them bit into their gooey sandwiches, causing a tasty ooze to trickle down their chins, eliciting smiles and giggles from both.

"You two look like you're having a messy, fun time!"

April tried to catch the marshmallow dripping from her mouth. "Hi Mrs. Thomas!"

"Hey Mom! Didn't know if you would make it."

"Of course." Surveying the festivities, she added, "I didn't want to miss what seems to be a great time. Thanks for inviting me."

"No problem."

To Kelsie, Jessie seemed genuinely glad to see her, which made her feel a bit more at ease. It was a good feeling that she would have liked to continue enjoying but, not wanting to cramp her son's style, she looked around as she continued. "Either of you know where Brice is?"

"Pretty sure I saw him with a group of people at the side of the DJ stage," April stated as Kelsie looked in the direction she was pointing.

"Thanks. You kids have fun." She turned to leave as she gave Jessie a wink. "I'll see you later." She smiled as she scanned the crowd near the stage for Brice, finally spotting him. As she walked over, she saw Kim talking with her son, who was definitely interested in the good looking young man they were standing with. They all seemed content, with their individual worries in each of their personal rear-view mirrors. Kelsie was happy for them.

Brice's back was facing her when Kelsie tapped his shoulder. As he turned, a happily surprised expression appeared on his face. "Well, good evening. This is a surprise!"

"Good evening to you too," Kelsie was thankful he was happy to see her. "Didn't Jessie tell you I was coming?"

He shook his head. "After I told him he could call to invite you, he never even mentioned whether or not he made the call."

"Well then, this really is a surprise." She laughed. "He was probably hoping I wouldn't come in case I embarrass him!'

"Most likely," said Brice as he gave her a wink and smiled. "But I'm glad you're here."

"I try to never miss a good time." She matched his smile. "Like last Saturday. Thanks for suggesting we all go for a ride."

"Happy you were up for it. And that you haven't lost your riding skills."

"I was a little surprised how it all came back to me."

"Like riding a bike."

"I guess so. But I had a great time, really." Her genuine smile reflected her sincerity. "Thanks again."

"I had fun too." He surprisingly felt uncharacteristically bashful as he looked at her with what he was certain was a goofy-looking smile that seemed to be plastered on his face.

"April seems very nice. And I think she might be helping Jessie to come out of his shell a bit."

Brice's expression changed slightly.

Damn, she cursed herself. *Did I change the subject too soon?? Was he wanting to continue talking about last weekend?* It had been so long since Kelsie was interested in someone new that she had forgotten how to let a conversation flow to determine if the other person shared a similar interest.

While she was still cursing herself, a former program participant came up to Brice to say "Hi" and thank him for his help. Kelsie tried not to be involved in their brief conversation and was happy Brice appeared to want to get back to the chat they had been having.

When Brice was finally able to turn back to her, Kelsie didn't notice the slightly concerned expression on his face. To him, Jessie needed to do a lot more work in order to get his life back on track and Brice wasn't thinking April was going to help much with that.

Kelsie was deep in thought as to how she could correct her earlier blunder when she came back to their conversation. "It felt good to ride again. I'm actually surprised you remembered that I rode back in high school."

He let out a slightly nervous chuckle, thankful to turn the conversation away from Jessie's progress, or possible lack thereof. "Well, *you* probably don't remember that I used to work at the stables where you took riding lessons."

"You were dependable enough to hold down a job back then?"

"Don't act so surprised. To be a successful juvenile delinquent, you need to have a little cash in your pocket."

Kelsie was embarrassed by her comment. "I'm sorry, that was rude of me to say. I just don't remember seeing you working there back then."

"No worries," he replied, knowing his reputation was a hard thing to circumvent. "I managed to be dependable enough hold that job all through high school, right up until we left."

"So what was it about that job that held your attention and kept you there?"

That wasn't a hard question for Brice to answer as he broke into a big smile. "The secret was I loved horses. I may not have had much of an affinity for learning in school, but back then I wanted to learn as much as possible about horses and be around them as much as I could." He reflected for several moments before continuing. "That job kept me out of trouble."

The disbelief on Kelsie's face was impossible to miss.

"OK, not completely out of trouble. But believe me, I would have been a lot worse off if it hadn't been for that job. It was the only constant, good thing in my life for a long time."

She sensed his mood could turn melancholy as he spoke about his job at the stables where she had spent a good portion of her youth, so Kelsie made an attempt to keep the evening more light-hearted. "I'm glad you were able to turn things around. And look where you ended up!" She held her arms out."You're doing a lot of good here. Not just for my son but I see a lot of satisfied, happy faces here tonight belonging to parents and kids alike. That might not be the case if you had continued to waste your life just because it started out rough. I think there are too many people in this world who could turn themselves around but don't, either because they don't have the opportunity or the desire to change. You should be proud of yourself."

"It was touch and go there for a while. It could have easily gone either way with me." He looked at her with appreciation in his eyes before continuing. "But you're right. I'm very proud of what I've accomplished and of what we accomplish here on a regular basis." He hoped she would feel the same way regardless of Jessie's success or failure in the program.

Silence fell between them as they stood together, surveying the party. Several people came up to shake Brice's hand and say "thank you". As they looked at Kelsie standing next to him, she smiled back, not offering anything to anyone. She was perfectly happy to appear as anything but the parent of a troubled teen, even if only for a few moments.

As the music pumped out of the speakers and the sounds of people having fun surrounded them, Brice asked, "Would you like to go to dinner one night this week?"

Kelsie was caught off-guard by his question, then broke into a broad smile. "Is the class bad-boy asking the bad hair and braces girl on a date?"

He laughed. "Don't get carried away. It's not like I'm asking you to wear my class ring around your neck." He almost added 'yet' to the end of his statement. He wasn't sure why.

"Remember when that was the ultimate thing?"

"Actually, I really don't. That part of the high school experience totally passed me by."

"That's too bad. I'm sorry you missed out on so much back then. But I'm happy to say yes to your dinner invitation!"

They both smiled, feeling as if they were back in high school and maybe getting a second chance at...something.

A light snow started to fall, making the festive atmosphere around them even more so.

Chapter Fourteen

The restaurant Brice chose was very much to Kelsie's liking. It was a small, quiet establishment, something she usually had a hard time finding. She hadn't had a dinner date since her husband's passing but even when she and Tina went to dinner, every place seemed so loud that it was hard to converse without being equally loud, which Kelsie was loathe to do. She hated being loud in public and didn't appreciate other's being that way. She wondered how new couples, who typically would get to know each other over dinner, were able to do so in a noisy restaurant. Shouting out personal details in a crowded space was not her style.

She appreciated the subtle lighting that was bright enough to read the menu but low enough to allow for an intimate evening. And the aromas coming from the direction of the kitchen were making her mouth water. She wasn't sure how Brice managed to determine Italian food was her favorite but she was glad of it, even if it was probably a happy coincidence.

As they settled into their seats and ordered drinks, Kelsie realized the ambiance surrounding her was the perfect setting for romance. She thought about how scary dating could be with all the craziness in the world and wondered just how people managed it as she realized, she was managing it herself at that moment.

"This place is very nice. Is it where you bring all your third dates?" To her surprise, she was suddenly feeling uncharacteristically flirty.

"Third date?" Brice looked at her quizzically. "How do you figure?"

Even though she was slightly uncomfortable with how she started the evening's conversation, she had no choice but to explain herself. "Coffee the first weekend, horseback riding last weekend, now dinner. That's three in my book."

Brice smiled. "Makes sense. But what about the bonfire?"

"Ahh, well, you didn't invite me to that. Jessie did. So you're still at three. Now, answer my question," she teased.

"Well, since I don't know that I've ever actually had a third date, I guess this is now officially my third-date, go-to restaurant."

"You don't expect me to believe you haven't had your share of third dates?" she queried.

"Nope. Pretty sure this is my first one."

"You were always pretty popular in school." She shot him a skeptical glance. "I'm thinking it was that "bad-boy" image you cultivated so well that got the girls attention." She stopped herself from blurting out 'including mine'.

He smiled. "Well, as you have pointed out before, it wasn't exactly an "image". I was pretty successful at being an actual bad-boy."

"Yes, you were. Glad to see that might have changed."

He winced. "I think you know by now it has."

Kelsie looked at her wine glass in silence as the waiter set it in front of her. When he had left the table, she finally spoke. "You're right. I'm sorry I said that."

"No need to apologize. The past is the past and it can't be changed." He paused, considering if he should dwell on past behavior or move on. He opted for the latter, wanting to bring a lighter tone to the evening. "But it really has been a long time since I've been on a third date. I was never any good at follow-through in school and that's one bad trait I haven't managed to alter."

Kelsie flashed him an irresistible smile. "Maybe I'm a good influence on you."

"Could be. It's always been a bit of a struggle for me to trust women who might be interested in starting a relationship. I tend to shut it down before anything develops. Hence, no third dates."

Kelsie thought it was odd he would self-destruct potential relationships. "Any idea why?"

"No clue," he shrugged. Yet he was well aware that his issue with trusting women stemmed from his mother leaving the family when he was so young. But he didn't want to delve into that heavy topic so instead he smiled at the very attractive woman with whom he was currently on a third date. "But I'm working on it."

Kelsie could see it in his eyes. He was different than the person she remembered from school. And she was glad of it. She had always felt a bit awkward regarding her attraction to him back then. Of course, it didn't matter at all once he disappeared so she hadn't thought about him in forever. But over the years, she had questioned some of the things she did and felt in her youth. Nothing specific; just in general. She knew she had done questionable things in her past. But she was thankful they didn't matter in the end. And she took Brice's change as a positive sign that, perhaps the attraction she felt then wasn't misplaced. It was just placed too soon.

The waiter arrived to take their appetizer order just at the right time. Brice smiled as Kelsie requested the bruschetta.

"I was going to order the same thing. It's my favorite."

"Mine too!" Kelsie hoped her response, which was a bit more enthusiastic than she had hoped, didn't make her sound like a giddy school girl trying to impress her date. She blushed.

Brice laughed and signaled to the waiter that they would take two orders. "I want to make sure you don't try to mooch anything off my plate!"

Kelsie feigned offense. "I would never!"

Brice laughed as he wondered if his affectionate glances might be giving away the feelings that were growing within him.

As they settled into their evening together, they were both thankful the conversation became easier, less stiff, like what takes place between friends getting to know each other better. Or two people on a *real* date. Except that Kelsie was certain it had been much longer since she had experienced a real date than it had been for him.

"So, are you set for Christmas?" he casually asked. "I imagine you are the type to go all out for the holiday."

"I do tend to overdo it sometimes," she admitted sheepishly. "But I really enjoy all the holiday prep. Shopping, decorating, baking, all of it."

His smile told her he was not at all surprised by her admission.

"Of course, it's not the same this year." A bit of sadness crept into her mood.

Brice knew what she meant so he didn't press, figuring she would expound on the statement if she felt like talking about it.

"As you can probably figure out, it's the first Christmas in 17 years that I'm preparing for completely alone. This has always been my favorite time of year but it's not much fun decorating and baking and all that without Jessie around. It feels weird not having to hide the gifts I've bought him. And I always buy him too much stuff so hiding everything has always been a challenge." She examined her half-empty wine glass. "But not this year."

"Sorry it's a difficult year for you." Brice reached for the bottle of wine on the table and refilled her glass. "But it's equally difficult for Jessie. I'm pretty sure he would rather be helping you lug out the decorations and put them up rather than being where he is." He smiled. "And believe me, no kid really likes lugging out decorations and putting lights on the house in the cold weather!"

His joke made Kelsie smile. "Believe it or not, Jessie has always been a big help to me at this time of year. He loves to help me decorate cookies and make the house festive." She laughed as she watched the appetizers being placed on the table while they spoke. "At least, that's how he's always made it seem. Could be that he was just helping so he'd get extra presents."

Brice held his wine glass up to toast. "Here's to extra presents."

"I'll drink to that!"

They smiled as their glasses came together, lightly making a clinking sound.

"But I honestly think it's his favorite time of year too. I'm really looking forward to him coming home."

For the first time that evening, Brice felt a bit awkward. He took a bite of the food before him so his silence didn't reveal his trepidation regarding Jessie's future.

Kelsie didn't catch the change in Brice's demeanor. "I know I probably shouldn't ask because I'm certain you like to keep your work with him separate from anything going on between us." She flashed him a sly smile before continuing. "But can you tell me anything official about how he's doing?"

Brice looked at his plate as he spoke. "I don't think it's something we should talk about here."

She immediately held her hands up in a gesture of surrender. "I'm so sorry! You're absolutely right! And I truly don't want to spoil this lovely dinner. I just can't help but worry about the progress he's making and if it's enough for the judge to consider. I know she'll be trusting your judgment." She looked at him squarely. "So am I."

The discomfort Brice was feeling was evident in his expression. It had to be. He had never perfected the art of hiding what he was feeling. And at that moment, he was feeling uncomfortable. Fortunately, the waiter arrived to take their dinner order. Kelsie decided on the special; Chicken Marsalis with a white wine sauce over angel hair pasta. Brice acted like he couldn't decide in order to buy himself some time, asking the waiter for his recommendation regarding one dish over the other. But he knew all along he was going with his favorite; Chicken Parmesan.

With the waiter gone, Brice wanted desperately to change the subject. But his mind went blank. Suddenly he couldn't think of something witty to say or some subject to offer up for discussion. He cursed himself. While he hadn't been on any third dates, he'd had his share of first and second ones so he didn't know why he couldn't figure out what to say! He knew he had to come up with something soon or Kelsie was going to continue prying about her son.

He looked across the table at an anxious face that likely wasn't going to give up on trying to get information out of him. This wasn't the direction he wanted the evening to be headed. "I'll be honest with you. I see potential in Jessie. Real potential. And I'm not just saying that because I'm having dinner with his mother at the moment. I'll say the same thing to the judge. He clearly has bonded with Bailey. And he and April seem to have a real connection. Perhaps more than just friends."

"I sense that too, especially after watching them together at the bonfire the other night," Kelsie agreed. "It's the first time I've seen him take more than a casual interest in a girl. And she seems very nice. In fact, everyone I've met in the program at Redemption is very nice. None of them seem like trouble makers, including April."

"You've caught us at a good time. Most of the kids we are helping at the moment aren't severe cases and we've been able to help them see their way toward a better path." He didn't bother to mention that April actually wasn't enrolled in their program.

"More success stories for Redemption!"

"Absolutely."

"And surely Jessie bonding with Bailey and April are good signs," Kelsie said as more of a statement than a question. "Seems like he's coming out of his shell and thinking of others. That's gotta be a good sign, right?

"Yes, I agree. There are good signs where Jessie is concerned. And like I said, I see real potential in him."

The pause in Brice's speech made Kelsie's heart sink.

"But..." she said.

"I'm going to be totally honest with you." He braced himself and spoke truthfully, as he always did when discussing a program participant, even when he knew what he was about to say would not be what the person at the other end of the conversation wanted to hear. "While Jessie is making progress, he hasn't, as of yet, made a breakthrough. I don't see an indication of any drastic changes in his overall attitude and demeanor. He still has anger inside him over losing his father and he simply can't understand why he suffered such a great loss."

"*We* suffered the loss together. I would think it should have brought us closer."

"Most times that does happen within families."

"So why does Jessie think that shutting me out and acting up is the way to deal with it?"

"Most likely because he can't figure out how to process it, how to make sense of it."

Kelsie looked at Brice with a blank expression. "But you're helping him with that, right?"

"Of course I'm trying to. But there is only so much I can do. We talk every day and I've had him working on various projects that should be helping him to know there are still good aspects to his life that he can appreciate and enjoy, even without his father at his side. He needs to realize that a change is needed within himself in order to change his situation. But so far, he's resisting making the changes he really needs. He's still angry about his father dying and he's having trouble figuring out what to do with his anger. He needs to want to make a change in his life. And from what I've seen so far, he just won't do it."

"Won't or can't?" Kelsie asked. "I thought your job was to help him figure out why he has so much anger about things he can't change. And to help him realize that if he doesn't change, he could end up in a place that I know would do him more harm than good!" She stopped talking as the realization of her words settled in her mind. She shuddered slightly.

"I don't disagree with you. Jesse doesn't need Juvenile Hall or a half-way house. He needs to be with you and his friends. But he needs to realize that only he has the power to change himself, to not act out when the anger inside him becomes too much. He needs to think about more than himself. But unfortunately, he hasn't gotten there yet. And I can't tell the judge he's changed if he truly hasn't. That's a disservice to him and to everyone around him."

Kelsie wasn't sure what to say. She could feel her face becoming flushed as she stared at the fork sitting next to her half-eaten appetizer. Finally, she looked up and spoke firmly. "Well, you simply need to make him realize what he needs to do!"

Just then, the waiter appeared at their table. No one spoke as the small plates were cleared away to make room for their entrees. While the food looked and smelled delicious as it sat in front of Kelsie and Brice, neither had an appetite any longer.

Brice finally spoke softly. "What you need to realize is that I can't *make* him do anything other than the steps of our program, which he is doing. But at this point, it's just not affecting real change in him."

"But I don't understand. You said he was making progress. I've seen that he's making progress! He lights up when he's around Bailey. I haven't seen him get excited about anything in a very long time." Kelsie's confusion grew the more she spoke. "He was actually proud of himself when he told me about Bailey being sick and how he stayed up all night to help him get better. He never shares things like that with me. He even called to invite me to the bonfire. I can tell he's changing, for the better! Why don't you see that?"

"Please understand that I do see it. But he's not making enough progress. He hasn't shown me that he's interested in making a true change within himself. He has to *want* to turn himself around. No matter how much you or I want that to happen, it's totally up to him."

Kelsie couldn't believe what she was hearing. She felt as though her only son was slipping away from her with every word Brice spoke. "Well maybe you need to change your tactics!"

Brice understood her frustration. It wasn't the first time he had delivered such a message to a disbelieving parent. But it had never happened over dinner. "Our program and the plan we have in place is the most successful within 100 miles of here. It works for the vast majority of the people who walk through our doors. People who have a multitude of different difficulties. They are people who want to be helped, who have hit the bottom and want to change before they fall even farther. Having a desire to be helped is essential. But, unfortunately, there are a few who can't be helped. Or don't want to be helped. It's a sad but real truth."

Brice regretted his choice of words quicker than the incredulous expression formed on Kelsie's face. Not because he didn't want to suffer her wrath but because he would typically form this particular truth a little more gently.

"So you think my son can't be helped?!? Really?" Kelsie was on the verge throwing her pasta at the man sitting across the table. "I trusted you, against my better judgment I have to say, to help my son, to bring him back to me! And you're giving up on him? He's only got one week left in the program and you're telling me he won't make it through?!?"

"Please calm down. I'm not saying anything for certain."

"That's not what I'm hearing!"

"Then you aren't listening." He couldn't suppress the frustrated edge in his voice. "I'm simply telling you that I haven't seen him make a significant breakthrough yet, one that will let me tell the judge that, in my professional experience, he will be able to deal with his feelings in the future and channel them into more positive outlets. That's what I need to see in order to help with his legal situation."

Kelsie slumped in her chair. "I should have known. I can't believe I started to think you had really changed from when we were in school." As difficult as it was, Kelsie kept her voice low, although she couldn't mask her growing rage. "You gave up on school, you give up on women before the third date and, true to form, now you are giving up on my son."

She removed the napkin from her lap and placed it on the table, then leaned in to emphasize her words. "You know he is all that I have and you're just going to let them take him away from me. I trusted you to help him, to bring him back to me, but instead, you're just giving up on him like you give up on everything in your life."

Kelsie stared at Brice for a moment, trying to calm down. He remained quiet, trying to determine if she was done and ready to let him explain further. Unfortunately, she wasn't.

"What if the person who set you on your current path had given up on you? Have you thought about that at all while you're giving up on my son?!?" She stood up and removed her coat from the back of her chair as she continued. "Maybe your mentor should have given up on you so you wouldn't have had the opportunity to be such a disappointment to Jessie...and me!"

As un-dramatically as she could manage, she left the restaurant, wanting to not draw attention to herself as tears streamed down her face. She couldn't get away from there fast enough. Once outside, she ran to her car as fast as she could. Inside, she cried like she hadn't cried since she suffered her last great loss. The evening, the week, the month had all started with great promise. And now she was crying her eyes out in her car outside of the restaurant where her world had come tumbling down...again

Brice sat at the table, trying to comprehend what had just transpired. He wanted nothing more than to go after Kelsie, to try and reassure her that what he told her didn't mean all was lost. As she had noted, Jessie still had a week left and there was no telling what might happen during that week. But he knew his words would fall on deaf ears. Ears which had already been tainted by everything he had said. He knew he should have changed the subject as soon and Kelsie asked about Jessie. But just like when they were in school, she made him nervous and he completely forgot all the things he knew he should do.

He mentally kicked himself as he paid the check for their untouched dinners and left.

Chapter Fifteen

The bus dropped everyone from Redemption off at the front door of a non-descript warehouse under skies that promised snow if the temperature remained steady. Max was first off the bus, eager to get started on the project that had been described to everyone in attendance as an important charity event. Those who followed Max showed varying degrees of interest, with April and Jessie the last to disembark as he was showing the least interest of anyone.

They quickly filed inside, mostly because they were cold, but the inside of the drafty warehouse didn't provide much relief. It was cold and un-inviting, even though as far as the eye could see, toys, games, clothing, books and more were stacked high. Jessie thought the contents of the building screamed "fun" but he didn't anticipate anything enjoyable coming out of his time there. But it was part of his punishment. At least, that's how he thought of it, even though he would be chastised severely if he dared speak the descriptive term aloud. However, he couldn't fathom any other way to look at it. He just wanted to get through the exercise so he could get back to the ranch and spend time with Bailey.

A few complaints were mumbled as everyone signed in, then gathered together in the entrance to the main part of facility where they received instructions from Hannah, the seemingly very organized, no-nonsense volunteer coordinator. Jessie figured that if she could, she would shoot a death-ray out of her eyes at anyone who dared to disrupt her training speech with a snide comment or any other type of chatter.

He had been half-heartedly listening to her at first, but something she said caught his ear. "In most cases, the families that sign up for our program can't afford to buy their family gifts for Christmas. Many can barely afford to put food on the table and pay the rent. So in just about every case, the items you place in the boxes you pack will be the only gifts these kids receive this year. So please take the time to examine the lists you get and do your best to fill each box with items that are desired by, and appropriate for, each child."

To Jessie, Hannah's statement didn't ring true. He couldn't fathom that there were parents who couldn't afford to buy gifts for their kids, even just one or two items.

Hannah continued her instructions as Jessie listened a bit more closely. "Make sure you gather a toy or game, at least one article of clothing and at least one book for each child. You can place up to six items in each box so if there aren't 6 items on the child's wish list, take a moment to think about what that child might like, based on what they have requested and the information you'll find on each wish-list. And most importantly, have fun with it!"

Have fun? Jessie thought. The whole exercise was depressing and, to him, still unbelievable. He looked at April as she smiled and nodded her head in agreement with Hannah's last statement.

"OK, does anyone have any questions?" Hannah queried as she looked at the 30 or so volunteers in front of her. She was happy to see a strong turnout for the afternoon shift as there was much to be done. Seeing no hands raised, she gave the command. "OK everyone, let's get going!" And with that, people started chattering and buzzing around the warehouse, in search of their first wish-list.

In what could have been total chaos, everything was surprisingly organized. Gift boxes that had been filled by the morning shift sat amongst the rows of tables containing empty boxes yet to be filled. Per Hannah's instructions, volunteers located empty boxes. Inside each one was a wish-list from a child along with their age, gender and clothing sizes. In most cases, there was also information about the child's hobbies, interests, what kind of books they liked, if they had a favorite subject in school and what sports they liked. All the information was provided to help each volunteer pick just the right gifts. Items in the warehouse were displayed in sections: toys in one area; games in another; books in another. Sporting equipment had a quarter of the warehouse dedicated to it and clothing took up almost half of the entire facility. Racks and bins containing coats, jeans, dresses, shoes, shirts and everything in-between were organized by size and gender for easy picking. And April seemed to know just what to do.

"You act like you've done this before." Jessie was surprised by her eagerness to get going.

"Actually, I *have* done this before," she replied. But before he could ask for details she didn't want to provide, she was off towards the game section as she studied the list she had obtained.

Jessie looked inside a box and retrieved its list. "This shouldn't be too hard," he mumbled as he moved toward the clothing area. He was aware of the people around him all seeming to be having...fun. He wondered what was going through their heads. He looked at the task as an assignment, something he had to get through so he could "graduate" from the Redemption program and go home. He wasn't sure he believed what Hannah had said about the gifts they were packing being the only things the kids would get for Christmas. *Whatever*, he told himself as he set about to complete the task and get out of there. He would rather be brushing Bailey.

He approached the sporting goods section and casually grabbed a bat, then walked over to the games and grabbed a hand-held video game, then wandered over to the clothing section. There were so many clothes that it was the only section of the warehouse where staff was standing by to help the volunteers find what they needed without making a mess of the organization that had taken so long to achieve.

"What are you needing?" said a smiling woman as Jessie approached.

Her cheerfulness was a little more than he wanted to endure but if she could make the process go any faster, he would take the help. "I need some clothes."

"That's what I figured," said Smiling Face, with a tinge of sarcasm. "Anything in particular?"

"I dunno. Give me a pair of jeans I guess."

"Can you tell me the gender, size, desired color, anything besides 'a pair of jeans'." Smiling Face was still smiling but not quite as vigorously.

Jessie looked at the list. "An 11 year old girl."

Smiling Face stopped smiling. "Let me see that," she said as she reached for the paper. "It says here this girl likes to read and would like a doll."

Jessie stared at her blankly.

Suddenly her smile turned into a frown. "Do you really think the items in your hands fill the request of this little girl?"

"Maybe she needs to broaden her horizons."

Jessie's snarky statement wasn't winning over the other person in the conversation.

"And maybe you need to take this a little more seriously."

Jessie clearly didn't care.

"You may have all the goodies you want in your life but not everyone is as fortunate. Whether you want to believe it or not, there are many people in this world who can't afford basic necessities so things like Christmas gifts are out of the question. So we try to put some unexpected but much needed joy into these people lives, people who may go through the entire year without experiencing any real joy. Can you imagine a year, a month or even a day where you have nothing to look forward to?"

Jessie could relate to her last statement. He hadn't felt any joy for a long time. But he did remember what it felt like to have it. So it was unthinkable to him that some people never have that feeling.

"Some people in this world barely get by, day to day. They're good people, people who work hard. But for whatever reason, they can't seem to get ahead. And all they want is to be able to give their children some happiness, even if they can only do it one day a year and only with the help of charities. So they sign up for programs like this and with the food bank down the street so that, for one day a year, their family can have a truly joyful Christmas. But a spoiled brat like you comes along and craps all over their happiness because you're too wrapped up in your own self-centered self that you can't even spend a few hours thinking about others and doing something nice for them!" She looked at him incredulously. "Why did you even come here today?"

Smiling Face was smiling no more as she turned towards the stacks of clothing and quickly picked out an appropriate sized pair of jeans, a nice stripped shirt, some socks and a warm coat, then forced them into Jessie's arms. "At least with these, I know she'll get *something* useful for Christmas." Then she turned away to leaving Jessie to ponder what she had said.

He moved away from clothing area and sat on the edge of a fixture holding stacks of books. He looked at the list and actually read it. The 11 year old girl did, in fact, like to read and provided a list of her favorite books. It also said that she wanted to be a Mechanical Engineer when she grows up. Jessie was impressed. He had no clue what he wanted to be when he was 11. He wasn't even sure he knew what he wanted to be now. He hadn't given much thought to what he would study in college and here was a girl 6 years younger than him who already knew what she wanted to do with her life.

Without being too obvious, Jessie put the baseball bat and video game back where he found them and walked over to the books and started looking for something he thought would be a good read for the young girl. Then he went over to the toy section. As he walked back to his box to fill it, April was finishing up her first box.

"Looks like you got some good stuff," she said as he approached with his arms full.

"I managed to find some things that will work." He started to place everything in the box, laying the clothes in the bottom and what he considered the fun stuff on top.

"Who's all this for?"

"An 11 year old girl."

April eyed Jessie suspiciously. "A model car, a Lego set and a copy of *Little Women?*"

"Yep."

"For an 11 year old girl?"

"That's right." Jessie looked very pleased with himself as he finished packing the box.

"Are you sure you're taking this seriously?"

"Absolutely!" He smiled as he explained his choices. "Her list says that she likes to read and wants to be a Mechanical Engineer. So I figure a model car that she has to assemble will help her see how things go together. And a Lego set will help her to figure *how* to make things go together. And from the description on the back of the book, it seems like it's an inspirational story for someone who doesn't have a lot. I'm hoping it might help her to figure out the best way to help herself."

April stared in disbelief at Jessie. She could have been knocked over with a feather. "Wow! I'm impressed you gave it that much thought!" She hadn't been sure Jessie was even capable of such thoughtfulness.

Jessie laughed. "Guess you're a bad influence on me." He was happy he surprised her, especially since it didn't seem as though he was benefitting very much from his time at Redemption.

The smile April beamed at him confirmed he had made the right gift choices. He had felt confident when he was picking them out but April's approval made him feel even better. Before she could say anything that might embarrass him, he reached into another box, retrieved the list and was off on a new hunt for gifts.

For several hours, Jessie, April and the others did their best to make Christmas wishes come true. While none of them would be able to see joy on the faces of the kids they were helping on Christmas morning, knowing what they were doing would bring smiles to young faces and the prospect of hope was inspiration enough to keep everyone working in the cold and crowded facility. No one bothered to take a break and when pizza was brought in, they paused for no more than a few minutes, just long enough to consume a slice or two before getting back to work. The goal was to fill as many boxes as possible and no one wanted to let down any kids.

Jessie and April kept working at a brisk pace, filling boxes with items on the wish lists and then adding something they thought would make the day extra special for each child. They took turns showing each other the specific items they chose, explaining each choice. Jessie even managed to bring the smile back to Smiling Face as he joked with her every time he came to pick up clothing for another child. "You're favorite spoiled brat is back for more," was a line he used on her more than once. The assignment turned out to be more fun, and rewarding, than he had ever imagined.

Hannah stepped onto a pedestal in the middle of the vast warehouse. "OK folks, you've done a great job but it's time for us to wrap things up. Thank you very much for filling so many boxes. If you all wrap up the box you're working on now, we'll call it a day."

"Race you to do one more?" April challenged Jessie.

"You're on!" He reached into a box and retrieved the list and examined it carefully.

"What did you get?" April queried.

Jessie stood in silence, staring at the paper with a pensive expression as he reread the words, multiple times.

"You OK?"

Suddenly, he threw the list back into the box and, without a word, ran out of the warehouse.

Chapter Sixteen

When her phone rang, Kelsie didn't need to look at it to know Tina was calling. She hadn't talked to her since she walked out on her dinner with Brice and she wasn't too keen on talking about it. She decided to deflect the conversation as she answered. "How was your dinner with "Mr. Wonderful"?"

"Well, it's too early to call him "Mr. Wonderful" yet but he's getting there pretty quickly!" an excited Tina proclaimed. "And how was your dinner?"

"I want to hear about yours first." Kelsie wanted to put off the inevitable as long as possible.

"Well, his choice of restaurant wasn't the best but, honestly, he had no way of knowing that I don't like seafood. But it happened to spark some great conversation because I found out early on that he's not crazy about it either. He didn't want me to think that he was indecisive, and he figured that most women love seafood, so he thought it was a safe bet. Turns out the only seafood we both like is lobster so it was probably a more expensive dinner than he was planning. But he was a great sport about it, especially after I offered to pay for mine."

"So the slightly rocky start got smoother?"

"Oh girl, it did indeed. We talked about so much. Turns out he loves to cook, which is good because you and I both know I can't boil water! He's very much an outdoor person and is looking forward to hiking some of the trails around here so naturally I volunteered to show him my favorites."

"Naturally!"

"He loves to ski too, which I've always wanted to try so I might finally have someone to teach me." Tina's excitement was infectious as she continued. "And, if you can believe it, he actually asked about me! He wanted to know what else I like to do and was genuinely interested in knowing about me! I can't remember the last date I had where the guy showed any real interest in learning about me."

Tina's evening obviously went better than her own but Kelsie was happy for her bestie.

"OK, so enough about my evening. Tell me about your dinner with Brice."

Kelsie hesitated. She really didn't want to relive the entire unpleasant event but it was unavoidable. "Let's just say your date went a whole lot better than mine."

"Oh honey, I'm so sorry." Tina's exuberance was quickly replaced by a sympathetic tone as she felt her friend's pain."What happened?"

She sighed. "It started out fine. We met at a wonderful restaurant that smelled delicious. We had drinks, a terrific appetizer and then I made the mistake of bringing up Jessie."

"That doesn't seem like an unusual topic of discussion, considering he is the reason you two are back in touch after all these years."

"You would think. But I made the mistake of asking how he was doing in regards to what Brice's report to the judge will show. You know, how he's changing, improving."

"Yeah," Tina's hesitated, "probably not good to ask about something he probably can't share."

"I wish I had thought it through before I opened my mouth." Kelsie agreed.

"Did you get anything out of him?"

"He basically told me his report won't be positive. He can't tell the judge Jessie is improving if he's not."

Tina was shocked. Based on everything Kelsie had told her after each visit, it sounded to her like he was making great strides. "I can't believe he's not improving at all." She was realizing Kelsie's positive reports were very likely biased.

"He didn't exactly say that. He just said he's not making *enough* progress. Apparently he's waiting for some sort of "breakthrough", whatever that means."

Silence fell between them as Tina wasn't exactly sure of what to say.

"So even though Jessie has several days left to go and could still have the "breakthrough" Brice is waiting for," Kelsie continued, "to make matters worse and probably kill any chance of a good report coming in at the last minute, I accused Brice of giving up on Jessie, just like he gave up on school."

"Ouch," Tina winced. "But harsh as that may be, it sounds accurate. Brice was never known for finishing anything when we knew him."

"Yeah, but I've been going over the conversation again and again and I wonder if I was too hard on him or jumped to an assumption too quickly."

"It doesn't sound like it to me. Don't over-analyze things and drive yourself crazy. You can't do that to yourself." Tina couldn't help but think that Kelsie's description of the events and her assertion that Brice had once again proven himself to be undependable was very likely accurate.

Kelsie sighed. "Go ahead and say it."

"You know I would never say "I told you so". But we know how he is...or was. And it doesn't sound as though he's changed."

Unfortunately, Kelsie couldn't disagree.

***

It was late in the morning by the time Jessie slinked quietly into Brice's office for their daily session. He hadn't slept much and wasn't looking forward to the meeting where he was certain Brice would ask about his sudden departure from the gift box packing project the previous day, knowing his daily actions were reported on fully. He simply didn't want to talk about it.

He hadn't even bothered with breakfast, for some reason deeming it unimportant that morning. During his mostly sleepless night, he had thought about things which he took for granted in his life, things that others might be missing in their lives. The list he came up with made him realize he might actually be spoiled, something he had never previously considered. The thought bothered him through the night.

Brice was, as usual, sitting behind his desk, reading one of the many papers that were perpetually covering his work surface. Jessie had often wondered what all the paperwork was for. He imagined it to be reports, budgets, articles that kept the staff up on the latest therapy techniques; all things that he would find tedious and boring. He may not have known what he wanted to do with his life but Jessie was certain of one thing: he didn't want to be trapped behind a desk. The thought of pouring over paperwork or staring at a computer screen all day was depressing to him on a morning when he was already feeling low. He flopped into a chair in the middle of the room without uttering a word.

"Mornin'," Brice said, expecting no response.

Jessie didn't disappoint, sitting quietly while staring at nothing.

"You OK?"

No response was offered.

"I hear you packed a lot of boxes yesterday and did a great job. Really put thought into what items to pack for each child. I'm proud of you."

The silence from Jessie was deafening.

"Then I hear you got upset."

Jessie shifted in his chair, uncomfortable with the pending discussion regarding his hasty exit from the warehouse. He hoped not being forthcoming might lead to Brice giving up on the subject. But he knew better.

"You wanna talk about it?"

Jessie's stare was locked on the table separating the chairs in the middle of the room, even though there was nothing on the table to stare at.

Brice quietly got up and came around his desk to sit opposite Jessie, whose stare remained fixed on the table, as if Brice's change in location within the room wasn't noticed.

"I believe you got upset after reading the wish list from a 7 year old girl, is that correct?"

Finally, Jessie nodded, almost imperceptibly.

"You want to tell me what upset you about the list?"

Once again, it seemed like Brice was talking to himself.

"C'mon Jessie, give talking about it a shot. You can't keep what's bothering you bottled up inside."

Finally, Jessie broke his silence. "What she asked for."

"What she asked for is what upset you? Not sure I understand. Was it something extravagant?"

Jessie shook his head and remained silent, even though Brice could sense he wanted to talk but just couldn't bring himself to start.

Brice thought it best to remain silent, letting whatever was bubbling up inside Jessie make its way out in its own time. He didn't have to wait long.

Jessie finally looked up with moisture welling up in eyes that combined a mixture of frustration and sadness in their stare. He opened his mouth to speak but nothing emerged. After a moment, he found his voice. "She asked for a warm blanket and a mouse trap," he stated quietly, with a quiver in his voice.

"So her request is what made you run out on the warehouse yesterday?"

Jessie nodded.

"Why? How did her wish list make you feel that you ran out?"

"How do you think I felt?"

"I honestly don't know. That's why I'm asking.'"

"She should have been asking for toys or a dress or a book or whatever. But instead, she asked for stuff that no kid should ever have to ask Santa for."

A tear rolled down Jessie's cheek as he spoke, his words making his emotions burst through in a rush. The single tear was quickly followed by another and soon, they were flowing freely. He felt no inclination to hide them as words started to spill forth from him in a torrent of frustration.

"I can't even imagine what kind of place she's living in that she would have to ask for a mouse trap for Christmas!"

Tears continued to stream down his face as he stared at Brice and continued. "And a warm blanket?!? C'mon, it's not right. It's just not right!"

Brice placed a box of tissues on the table. "It's very unfortunate that some people live in less than ideal conditions."

"I think it's a whole lot more than "very unfortunate"." Jessie felt Brice was a little too casual in his statement.

"You're right, it is." Brice watched Jessie as his tears slowed. Yet frustration was still prevalent in his demeanor. "But that's reality for some people. Too many people, actually. There are many who can barely afford basic necessities and some who can't afford them at all."

Jessie was quiet as he started to realize more and more about the world he had never truly considered.

"What was it about a request for a blanket and a mouse trap that made you leave instead of trying to do something for that little girl?"

An expression of disbelief covered Jessie face. "What was I going to do? Give her a doll when she needs a whole lot more than that? Pretty sure there weren't a whole lot of mouse traps being gift-wrapped in that warehouse."

"True. But you could have packed a coat to keep her warm, a toy to make her smile and a book to help her escape her reality, even if she could only escape it in her mind."

Jessie looked at Brice sitting calmly across from him. He hadn't thought about doing any of that. His only thought after reading the wish list was he wanted to get out of there. *What's the sense in all of this?* he had asked himself as he ran through the warehouse door. His head was full of questions. "If I had done any of that, it wouldn't have changed the fact that she had to ask for a mouse trap and a blanket for Christmas and no one should have to do that, plain and simple."

"You're right, no one should. You've certainly never had to put things like that on your Christmas list, right?"

Brice's question was met with a menacing glare.

"We've talked about how fortunate you are, even if lately you don't feel that way. But there are most certainly a whole lot of people who are in worse situations than you. Believe it or not, despite the tremendous loss of your father, your situation is better than most."

"Is that supposed to somehow make me feel better about any of this?"

"Absolutely not! But it's a sad fact, one that should help those of us who are more fortunate to appreciate what we have and learn about what we can do to help others. After all, helping others was the goal of yesterday's project."

Overwhelming sadness hit Jessie. "And I couldn't even do that because I got too upset to pack a box with what she wanted."

"Well, as we know, you wouldn't have found what she asked for on the shelves."

Jessie contemplated Brice's comments. "But I should've done something."

"Well, it's not too late. Even if that box has been filled by someone, there are others to be done. I can take you there now."

Jessie became quiet as he considered the options available to him. Finally, he looked up and spoke with determination. "I want to find *that* box. Can we stop in town on the way to the warehouse?"

"What for?"

"I want to buy the things she asked for and put them along with a bunch of other stuff, fun stuff, in the box for her. I want her to be happy on Christmas morning and for as long as possible afterwards."

"Sounds like a great idea to me." Brice smiled as he got up and grabbed his coat. "I'll drive."

Jessie didn't crack a smile at the lame joke. He had a look of determination on his face that Brice had previously not seen on his young charge. *Maybe there's hope for this kid after all,* he thought to himself as he watched Jessie run to his room to retrieve his wallet and coat.

Chapter Seventeen

The day Jessie and Kelsie had been dreading finally arrived. Neither was sure how they would handle the outcome regardless of what it was. But they had to face the music. Kelsie was glad to have April in the courtroom with her since Tina wasn't able to be there. Having someone sitting with her, even if she didn't know her well, provided a measure of comfort. And since Kelsie had a dreadful feeling as to what the result of the proceedings would be, she knew she'd appreciate a familiar face nearby.

April had arrived with Brice. Fortunately for Kelsie, he had to sit in a separate section due to his involvement in the proceedings so no words were exchanged between them. Her disappointment in him had not waned since their unsuccessful third date.

On Christmas Eve, Kelsie was saddened to see the courtroom was so busy. Her stomached churned as the bailiff called the next case; Jessie's.

The judge referred to the folder in front of her. "Mr. Turner, would you please come forward so we can over the details of your report?"

Brice moved to the front of the courtroom and sat in the witness stand at the side of the judge's bench.

As Judge Cooper started the formal proceedings, Jessie could do nothing but watch his fate be influenced by one person at the front of the courtroom and decided by the other. The despair he felt was apparent on his face and his hands began to sweat as the judge started to address Brice.

"It's been 30 days so I assume Mr. Thomas has completed your program," the judge stated flatly.

"Yes, your Honor," Brice replied just as flatly.

Judge Cooper glanced over the report that Brice had submitted then looked at Jessie sitting next to his lawyer before continuing to address Brice. "Well, I've read over your report but could you please summarize it for us regarding Jessie's current frame of mind and the results of his participation in your program?"

"Certainly." Brice seemed prepared to give what, as far as Kelsie could determine, would be a less-than-positive report. "I am being totally honest when I say this was truly a difficult case. Jessie clearly misses the relationship he had with his father, which is understandable since it's obvious to me the relationship was a very strong one. I don't often run across young men who are fortunate enough to have a completely positive paternal relationship. It's that relationship which kept Jessie focused on positive things in his life, of which there are many. But with the loss of his father, Jessie has lost his compass in life. The loss has been an unbearable burden on him and therefore we've seen him acting negatively. Unfortunately, when that strong paternal relationship goes away, all too often I've see young men who have lost their direction, causing them to become angry at anything and everything. They also act out in ways to attract attention, even if it's negative. Jessie is, unfortunately, a classic case."

"But he completed your program?" the judge inquired.

"Yes, he did," Brice continued. "But completion doesn't always mean success. Sometimes I believe more time at our facility could help but in Jessie's case, I think that 30 days was enough to determine Jessie's frame of mind and what he needs."

"So what is your conclusion?" Judge Cooper was unsure of where Brice was heading with his report but eager to find out.

Brice glanced briefly at Kelsie as he began his response. "While Jessie does still have a loving, devoted parent and lives in a strong home environment, he has made some wrong decisions in the last 18 months, clearly not thinking or caring about the potential consequences."

Kelsie watched him reporting on her son while she seethed inside. She knew Brice was about to say something that would give the judge no choice but to put Jessie in some sort of situation she was certain would do him more harm than anything and do nothing more than continue to promote his downward spiral. She knew he needed another "last" chance but it was about to slip away. She wanted so badly to stand up and say something, beg the judge for leniency. But she knew if she did, it would most likely make things even worse, as if that were possible. She didn't want to hear it but she knew she had to fully concentrate on everything Brice was saying, in case she had an opportunity to refute him at some point.

Brice cleared his throat and continued his testimony. "As Jessie spent more time with us, I became absolutely certain that his detrimental behavior would continue and there was no way I could come here today and, with a clear conscious, recommend something other than Juvenile Hall or at least a half-way house with daily therapy sessions for several months."

It took every bit of restraint Kelsie could muster to keep herself from leaping out of her seat in an attempt to stop Brice from continuing. She felt as though the walls were closing in around her.

April slowly moved her hand and placed it on top of the fist that had formed on Kelsie's hand, hoping to calm her down.

"Then, something unexpected happened," Brice continued. "I'm sure you'll read the details in my report if you haven't already but the bottom line is, I feel certain that Jessie made real progress during his time with us, progress I didn't even realize he was making at times. And in my professional opinion, I think that with continued counseling, which I'm happy to provide, it would actually be detrimental to his well-being to lock him up. I truly feel his days of questionable decisions are behind him."

Judge Cooper looked directly at Jessie. "I think I'd call his decisions something other than "questionable" but I thank you for your testimony, your report and for your time." She turned to Jessie's lawyer, who had a somewhat stunned look in his eyes. "Mr. Olsson, do you have any questions for Mr. Turner?"

It took William a moment to realize the situation in which he found himself and his client. He quickly stood up. "No, your honor. Thank you, your honor." Just as quickly, he returned to his seat.

Judge Cooper turned her attention back to Brice. "Thank you again, Mr. Turner. You may step down."

Brice walked back to his seat, winking at Jessie while not glancing in Kelsie's direction.

Conversely, Kelsie couldn't take her eyes off Brice. She hoped he would see relief and gratitude in her expression. But she also was trying to figure out what happened. Her last conversation with him gave every indication that his testimony before the judge would have been nothing like what she had just witnessed. Tears started to well up in her eyes.

The judge looked at Brice's report briefly one last time, placed it on her bench and folded her hands on top of the folder. "I actually have read the entire report and it was indeed, very enlightening." Judge Cooper turned her demanding stare to Jessie as she continued to speak. "Young man, I'm truly pleased that my original assessment of what was best for you seems to have been correct. And I'm thankful that Mr. Turner was able to dig into whatever was working against you and help you to, at least, get a start on turning things around. According to his report, you've done a great deal of work on yourself, work that you may not yet even recognize you've done. But that's OK. One day soon, I think you will. And so does Mr. Turner."

She leaned forward in a successful attempt to properly emphasize her final words. "And I'm confident now that you'll continue to work on yourself, improve yourself, because we are all a work-in-progress."

Jessie stared at the judge, not fully comprehending what was happening. But he was starting to feel positive about his life for the first time in a long while.

Judge Cooper was about to give a ruling she enjoyed giving but didn't get to do often enough. "So it looks like Christmas has come a day early for you, young man. I'm ordering you to continue meeting with Mr. Turner at least twice a week, more if he deems it necessary, for the next 3 months as part of a one-year probationary period. Since you are under 18, if you stay completely out of trouble during that time period and appreciate the opportunity for the fresh start that you are being given, your record will be clean and you will not have to worry about your youthful indiscretions following you around for the rest of your life."

Jessie sat in stunned surprise, not wanting to breathe in case it broke whatever spell he felt he was under.

Kelsie was having a similar reaction.

Judge Cooper had one final comment. "I hope you'll determine a way to make yourself worthy of this opportunity so you can make a positive impact on this world and the people around you."

Jessie couldn't quite believe what had just happened. The court procedure had gone better than he'd ever dreamed possible. He suddenly felt as though his life was starting to move in the right direction, one that would make his father proud.

Kelsie could barely contain herself. But she knew nothing was final until the gavel fell. She held her breath as the judge continued.

"And one more thing…have a very Merry Christmas!" With that, her gavel came down and it was official. Jessie could come home!

"Thank you, your honor," William stood as he spoke, barely having uttered more than a few words during the entire proceeding.

"Yes, your Honor. Thank you, your Honor." Jessie could barely speak clearly as the words of gratitude fell from his lips. Overwhelming relief flooded through him as he shook William's hand vigorously until Kelsie ran over and gave him the tightest hug he'd ever felt.

"Thank you so much William," Kelsie said as she shook the lawyer's hand.

"Don't thank me, thank him," he said, pointing to Brice who was still seated. "He's the one that convinced the judge. This is probably the first time I've never had to do anything during a court proceeding." He winked as he added, "I'll feel guilty sending you a bill."

Jessie quickly came around the gate to hug April as they walked out of the courtroom with their arms around each other and a slight skip in their steps.

Kelsie followed them, smiling, her heart feeling lighter than it had since…she couldn't remember.

The hallway outside the courtroom was buzzing with people but Kelsie didn't notice anything. Her son was coming home for Christmas! That was the only thing that mattered to her on Christmas Eve. As they stood together smiling and hugging each other again, Brice approached the group, somewhat hesitantly.

April pulled slightly at Jessie and they moved away from Kelsie and Brice, giving them a moment of privacy she intuitively felt they needed.

Kelsie looked at Brice with grateful eyes as she struggled to find the right words. "I'm not sure what to say other than thank you."

"No need to thank me. I'm happy to give these types of reports."

"A report that was totally surprising to me," Kelsie admitted freely. "Can I ask what changed since we last spoke?"

"That's simple. Jessie changed," Brice stated matter-of-factly. "He finally realized he didn't have as much to be angry about as he thought."

Kelsie's expression reflected the question on her mind.

"Initially, I was concentrating on Jessie's lack of a strong male presence in his life since his father's death. I was certain it was the reason for his antics. And I wasn't wrong. He definitely misses having a guy to talk to about things and since he had such a great relationship with his dad, that's a tough hole to fill. But he eventually came to realize that he still has a strong mother he can lean on and even though he wasn't thinking of you as someone who could understand him like his father did, he finally got it through his head that he can."

Kelsie was surprised by his statement. She was certain his opinion of her had been severely tarnished by their dinner-date fiasco. Her expression reflected appreciation as he continued.

"Then he had occasion to realize something else that's very important. You can talk to him about it this evening and then hopefully have a nice Christmas tomorrow." He smiled at Kelsie and winked. "Hopefully Santa brings you something nice."

She felt flush as she smiled. "I already got what I want for Christmas," she said softly as she looked at Jessie talking to April. "You gave me my son back."

"He's the one that did the work. Just glad I could help facilitate things."

"Well, I still owe you a huge apology. I accused you of still being the guy I knew in school who gave up on everything when clearly you have come a long way. I truly am sorry."

Before Brice could figure out what to say, Jessie came over and vigorously shook his hand. "Thanks very much Brice. I really appreciate all you've done for me."

"All I did was help you to realize how to deal with everything that's going on, especially the stuff you have no control over. You did all the hard work. But hopefully now you know how to work with the stuff you can control and how to deal with the stuff you can't." The smile on his face reflected just how proud he was of his recent graduate. "I'm proud to have helped you figure things out."

Brice wanted to speak to Kelsie more but she was wrapped up in a celebratory hug with her now unencumbered son. He wasn't about to interrupt their celebration. Anything he needed to say could wait.

Chapter Eighteen

Christmas morning at the Thomas house was just as Kelsie had been hoping for…praying for. She awoke with a fresh perspective on her life. The previous day's events had proven to her that there was hope, even though the 18 months leading up to that morning had been terribly difficult for both her and Jessie. Up until the judge's gavel had fallen and they walked out of the courtroom together, she had felt like her life was on pause.

After asking him about his experience at Redemption late on Christmas Eve, Kelsie listened with great focus, trying to gather details regarding the "breakthrough" Brice had mentioned. Jessie hadn't been overly-eager to recount all the details. He mostly concentrated on telling her about Bailey, a bit about his roommate and something about a volunteer event where he and other kids packed gifts for families down on their luck. And he talked about April a lot, always with a smile on his face. Which made Kelsie smile.

Now, as she watched a light snowfall through her bedroom window on a cold, crisp Christmas morning, she truly felt that miracles do happen.

She got out of bed and put on her favorite fluffy, soft robe. It had been a gift from her husband the year they moved back to her hometown, where winters and Christmas days were properly cold. She could still feel his strength around her when she wore it.

Not hearing any movement from Jessie's room, she peaked in to find him still fast asleep. Long past were the Christmas mornings when he would be bouncing on his parent's bed at 6 am with excited anticipation of what Santa had brought. Being older, he still got excited, just not "6 am excited". And she figured since he probably hadn't slept much the night before his hearing, she decided to let him sleep as long as he wanted. The gifts under the tree weren't going anywhere.

And neither was he. That thought warmed her as she eased his bedroom door closed as quietly as she could.

With the coffee brewing, Kelsie turned on the tree lights and put on some Christmas music. She realized she had yet to play any of her favorite holiday tunes. She just hadn't felt like it was the Christmas season until it was almost over. She hadn't even done much decorating, unlike past years when some sort of Christmas decoration was tucked into just about every nook and cranny in the house. With the situation she had found herself in during the weeks leading up to the holiday, she hadn't been able to muster up the "Christmas spirit" so holiday cheer was lacking as she looked around the room. But she had managed to decorate the tree, which she found herself staring at as she sat on the couch.

As she relaxed for a few moments, one of her favorite songs, *Merry Christmas Darling*, started to play. The lyrics, about missing a loved one at Christmas, now took on a special meaning for her. She wished beyond measure that Steve was by her side. They had so many plans for their life together. But she realized she was fortunate to have had the time they did have together, regardless of how short it was.

Before she realized it, tears were streaming down her cheeks. She quickly realized they weren't tears of regret and sadness; they were tears of joy and appreciation. She knew Steve would not want her to be longing for him forever. He had told her as much before he passed. And now that she was finally able to breathe again after receiving the only gift she wanted for Christmas, maybe it was time to give serious consideration to his wish for her. Brice had been a first, although unplanned, attempt at something. She hoped her next attempt would go more smoothly.

She wasn't certain how long she sat there crying but she eventually realized she was hungry. And she assumed Jessie would be as well when he awoke, imagining the food he had been eating for the last 30 days wasn't anything like what he was used to.

She dried her smiling eyes and walked into the kitchen to start breakfast. She loved that the layout of their house allowed her to see the tree from the kitchen, its twinkling lights and festive decorations adding to the joy she felt that special morning.

The smell of bacon was the best thing Jessie could have imagined waking up to after the previous 30 days. He never really had a restful night at Redemption, even though the bed had been surprisingly comfortable. And while the food there was decent, no one made bacon with a proper crispy texture the way his mother did.

He opened his eyes and smiled when he confirmed the previous day hadn't been a dream. He was in his own room! Crawling out of his bed, Jessie put on comfortable sweats and made his way to the kitchen.

Kelsie didn't need to turn around to know her son was in the room. She easily sensed his presence and she loved the feeling. "Merry Christmas sleepy head."

"Merry Christmas best-mom-in-the-world."

"You're only saying that because it's true!" She turned and gave him a wink.

He stuck his nose over her shoulder as she stood at the stove. "That smells amazing. No one makes bacon the way you do."

"Figured I would start your first day of the rest of your life off right."

"'Preciate it."

"You want to eat or see what Santa brought you first?"

His eyes rolled. "Mom, I know Santa's not real by now."

"Who spilled the beans?!?" she exclaimed as they both laughed.

Jessie looked at all the gifts under the tree. Clearly his mother had gone overboard…again. "But if he was real, I'd say he made a mistake."

"How's that?"

"I wasn't so good that there should be so many gifts under the tree. Hope some of that is stuff you bought for yourself since I couldn't get you anything this year."

"They're all for you." she admitted sheepishly.

"That's crazy." He stared at the huge pile of perfectly wrapped presents. He was always impressed at how his mother wrapped gifts so perfectly.

"I did buy a few more things than I had originally planned," she acknowledged. "But every time I thought about you being at Redemption or, even more unthinkably, possibly not coming home, I'd get upset and buy you something else. It felt like I was *willing* you to coming home since you had so many gifts you needed to open."

He smiled at his mother, truly regretting what he had put her through. "I guess it worked."

"Indeed it did!"

He took a piece of bacon from a pile fresh off the frying pan. The texture was just the way he remembered it. "So, I kinda had an idea last night that I want to run by you."

"I'm all ears. You want 2 eggs or three?"

"Three please."

He watched as she cracked them into the pan and started the toaster.

"All the gifts you bought me…I just want you to know that I appreciate them very much."

She looked at his quizzically. "You don't even know what you got yet."

"I don't need to open the packages to know that everything under that tree is perfect for me." He took another look at all the colorful boxes. "But…"

"Yes…what is it?"

"You know that family shelter over on Maple Street?"

"Of course."

Jessie was surprisingly nervous as he spoke. "What do you think about taking my gifts to the shelter and giving them to the kids who are there?"

Kelsie looked at her son, wondering how it was that he had changed so much in such a short period of time. He had never really been a deeply thoughtful person. So the question he had just posed to her was not something she would have ever expected to hear from him.

She thought about it for several moments before replying. "That's a wonderful gesture but may I ask why you want to give up everything? There are a few things under there I'm pretty sure you'll really like."

"I'm sure I would. But I'm even more certain there are kids at that shelter who would like them more. And in a way, they probably *need* them more. They deserve a fun Christmas too."

Kelsie took a minute to appreciate his thoughtfulness and generosity before she responded by breaking out in a broad grin as she tried to control the tear that was desperately trying to fall from her eye. "I think that's an absolutely fantastic idea. I agree that those kids deserve a fun Christmas."

"Cool. Thanks Mom."

"After we eat, I can tell you which gifts should go to a boy and which ones would be appreciated by a girl."

Jessie only had to think about her comment for a moment. "Pretty sure we don't need to segregate them by boy/girl. Lots of girls like the same things boys like."

When did he get so insightful? Kelsie wondered. *Maybe Brice and his program really do perform miracles.*

"Indeed they do," she said. "So let's get this loot loaded up...right after we eat."

***

It took Kelsie and Jessie longer than she thought it would to get all the gifts loaded and unloaded from her car. She wondered how she had originally had been able to get everything home. Every inch of the car seemed to have a festive gift tucked into it.

When they arrived at the shelter and told the people in charge what they hoped to do, the reception to Jessie's idea was overwhelming. And with the gifts distributed and opened, every recipient was truly appreciative of what they received.

Jessie swelled with pride as he watched the growing smiles on faces of families who had only wanted safe shelter for Christmas, just like another family had wanted on the first Christmas so long ago. And now these families had a bit more. He knew no one was there because they wanted to be. They had to be there for their own good, much like he had to be at Redemption for his own good. He hoped the kids he was watching as they enjoyed the gifts meant for him would get as much from their time at the shelter as he did from where he had been living up until the previous day. Sitting amongst all the festivity he came to the realization that where you are living isn't as important as how you conduct your life.

As Kelsie and Jessie bid goodbye to everyone at the shelter and walked to their car, Kelsie beamed at her son. "You just gave those kids a much better Christmas than any of them could have hoped to experience this year. Perhaps it was even better than several of their prior ones". She hooked her arm through his as they walked. "I'm so proud of you, for so many reasons."

Jessie smiled as they got into the car. He felt a great sense of accomplishment as they left shelter parking lot. And he realized as he watched the snow continue to fall through the passenger window that he finally felt at peace.

Chapter Nineteen

It had been a hectic Christmas day and Kelsie was thankful for a few quiet minutes to reflect. After their eventful morning, she spent over an hour talking with her parents and sister, whom they were visiting. For years, Kelsie and her younger sister traded the holidays with their parents. This year it was Kelsie's turn to have them for Thanksgiving and her sister's turn at Christmas. Next year, they would reverse the holidays. Kelsie was thankful her parents were healthy and fit enough to make yearly trips to her sister's house several hours away.

Of course, everyone was thrilled when they learned of the judge's decision as her mother proclaimed her Christmas prayers had been answered. Kelsie's father spent several minutes talking to Jessie, which brought a smile and several belly-laughs to her son, who had most certainly changed during his time away. *Maybe Brice really does know what he's doing,* she had contemplated while watching Jessie on the phone with his grandfather.

And right after she hung up the phone, Tina called.

"What are you doing call me? You should be wrapped up in "Mr. Wonderful's" arms underneath your tree!"

"Girl, it's a little too soon to be wrapped up under his tree. But I'm cooking up some spectacular plans for New Year's Eve!" Her smile could almost be heard through the phone. "And stop calling him that! You'll end up using that instead of his name when you meet him."

"And just when will that be? I still need to provide my stamp of approval."

"You'll get your chance soon enough. We have a nice New Years Eve planned. If it goes as well as I've planned, you'll meet him very soon in the New Year."

"Looking forward to it."

"Now that he's home, what are you and Jessie doing for New Year's?"

Kelsie realized she hadn't thought to plan anything past Christmas. They had always spent New Year's at home when Steve was alive, preferring to welcome the New Year with a quiet celebration. She started thinking it might be a good year to break that tradition.

"I'm not certain. But I have a few ideas I think I'll run past Jessie."

"Good! I hope you two do something fun. You both deserve it."

"I think you're right," Kelsie agreed. "You wanna come over for some eggnog and cookies?"

"I thought you didn't make any cookies this year."

"I hadn't planned to but just in case Jessie came home, I had to make his favorite pecan logs. That's about all I made but they came out great."

Tina was sitting on her couch rubbing her feet. "I'd love to honey but I am beat. Gary made me the most wonderful dinner and then we went for a long walk and managed to get into a snowball battle, which I won, of course..."

"Of course."

"... then we watched *The Holiday* and then I came home. So I'm gonna take a nice, hot bath and go to bed."

"Sounds like you had a great Christmas. I'm really happy for you."

"Me too," Tina giggled. "I'll call you tomorrow. Goodnight."

"Goodnight. Merry Christmas!"

"Merry Christmas!"

Kelsie put her phone down as a thought churned in her head. Tina was right; she and Jessie deserved to do something fun for New Year's. She hoped he would be up for an adventure with his mother. But at the moment, she wasn't certain of what that adventure might be.

She sat for a while, staring at the tree and thinking while music played softly. Several times she picked up her phone, only to put it down a few seconds later without punching in a number. Finally, after several attempts, she placed a call.

*****

Brice was sitting on his couch, wishing he wasn't alone again on Christmas when his phone rang. He smiled when he read the caller ID.

"Merry Christmas!" His surprise was evident.

"Sorry to call you so late on Christmas. I'm sure you have better things to do than talk to me."

"Actually, I don't. But I didn't think I'd ever hear from you again so this must be some sort of Christmas miracle."

Kelsie paused at his response, not sure of any hidden meaning that might be contained within. She hoped making the call wasn't a mistake as she finally spoke. "Well, I'm sitting in front of my tree just thinking about how different this Christmas would have been without your efforts. I really wanted to thank you again."

Brice didn't say anything. It always embarrassed him when parents credited him with the changes they saw in their son or daughter. He knew the kids were the ones doing the work and making changes in their lives. He was simply a facilitator.

With no response forthcoming, she took a deep breath before nervously continuing. "So I thought I'd call on Christmas to see if there is any chance we could get back on the track we were on before I put my foot in my mouth?"

"And what track was that?" he teased.

She didn't want to blurt out anything that might scare him off so she chose her words carefully while making her meaning clear. "A track where I hope we travel in a similar path forward and see more of each other."

"Oh, *that* track," he responded. "I'm thinking there is a distinct possibility we could make that happen." He let the thought hang between them for a moment before continuing. "Just promise we'll be moving forward and not dwelling on the past."

Kelsie smiled as the nervousness she had been feeling in the pit of her stomach before making her call dissipated. "I think I can handle that."

Brice was relieved. He had really been hoping they could continue to build something between them but watched it all fall apart at their failed dinner. *Things are looking up!* he told himself.

Kelsie thought there was no better time to get started on rebuilding their relationship than that moment. "Did you have a nice Christmas?"

"I did, thanks. It's was pretty quiet around here so I took a nice, long ride on Bailey."

"How's he doing?"

"Very well. Jessie did a great job getting him to trust people. I think Bailey misses him."

"I know the feeling." She made a mental note to ask Jessie if he'd like to visit Bailey soon, figuring it wouldn't look too obvious that she wanted to see Brice if she *had* to take her son out to see his favorite horse. The thought made her smile.

"But it sounds like your Christmas was a bit lonely."

"Not at all," he countered. "I'm pretty busy all year long so on Christmas, I like to reflect on what I did right through the year, think about what I could have done better and generally take stock of my life and what I'm doing with it. A nice, quiet ride on a majestic animal like Bailey helps me to do that."

The depth of his answer surprised her. "Actually, that sounds like a great way to spend the holiday."

"I'm thinking your holiday was a lot different."

"Well, it was different than I thought it might be but it was just the way I wanted it to be." She explained Jessie's desire to donate all his gifts to the shelter and how much joy it appeared to bring to the people temporarily residing there.

He was impressed as Kelsie imparted the story. For much of his time there, Brice had truly felt as though Jessie would likely not make his way out of Redemption in the way Kelsie hoped but he had been surprised at how quickly things had turned around. "Looks like he got more out of his time here than even I thought."

"Seems like it was just what he needed. I'm so thankful, for several reasons."

He smiled at the thought that she was hopefully referring to more than just the reversal of her son's situation.

"Do you have similarly quiet plans for New Year's?" She hoped that she didn't sound as though she was fishing for an invitation to ring in the New Year together, even though that might have been exactly she was hoping for.

"Definitely not! My traditional New Year's celebration is much more active!"

Her thoughts of celebrating together were quickly dashed but she didn't let it sidetrack their conversation. "Don't tell me you go crazy in Times Square or something like that."

He let out a hearty laugh. "You flatter me if you think I can still party like they do in a place like that!"

"I seem to recall you and Bill were known for the parties you would throw!"

"Yeah, well, those days are gone. But I still manage to have a great time skiing with my niece at Mont Sutton in Canada."

"You ski?" She had never thought of him as particularly athletic when they were in school. But he did have a trim physic so it made sense that we kept active.

"Not often enough but I make sure I go at least once a year. Do you ski?"

"It's been a few years but we used to go every year. I've never been to Sutton though."

"It's a great mountain that's not overly popular so we can always get some nice runs in."

"Sounds like a great way to ring in the New Year." Kelsie had briefly hoped he might suggest they all go skiing sometime but realized it was very presumptuous. They hadn't even had a full third date yet!

"I look forward to it every year."

"As you should. You deserve a chance to rest and recharge. I hope you have a great time."

"Thanks. I hope you have a great New Year's too." He paused, feeling he shouldn't say more. But then he did. "I'm hoping we can get together when I get back. I think we have a third date to complete."

The smile that appeared on Kelsie's face said it all. But he couldn't see it so once she finally felt she could speak without sounding like an overly-excited schoolgirl, she eked out a response trying to sound calm. "I'd like that very much."

His smile suddenly matched hers. "Merry Christmas Kelsie."

"Merry Christmas Brice." Her smile didn't fade as she ended the call while an idea formed in her head.

***

Brice stared at his phone with a smile. He may have hoped, but he never expected, that he would hear from Kelsie anytime soon. Her call turned out to be the best Christmas gift he could have imagined. Whatever might happen between them down the road, he was thankful to at least have a chance to get things back to where he hoped they had been heading.

Christmas is a time for miracles he thought.

Brice sat and contemplated something Kelsie had said to him not long ago. He hadn't talked to his high-school friend in years but after she first mentioned him, Brice had given serious thought to calling his old buddy. Enough that he had looked up Bill's number. But it never happened. And now after talking with Kelsie and seemingly patching things up between them, he wondered if she was right that he and Bill might be able to bury their past differences.

Christmas is a time for miracles he thought again. Then, before he lost his nerve, he dialed the number.

He heard several rings before the call was answered. "Merry Christmas!" came a cheerful voice through his phone.

Memories suddenly flooded back to Brice as his heart started beating faster. He was speechless and starting to rethink his impulsive call.

"Hello?" the familiar voice said, trying to ascertain if anyone was on the other end.

"Hey Bill, its Brice," was all he could muster, uncertain what he would possibly say next.

There was a long pause. *Guess Bill's all out of holiday cheer,* Brice told himself as he prepared for the line to go dead.

"Now there is a voice I never thought I'd hear again." Bill said quietly.

"More like a voice you never *wanted* to hear again?"

"Not true." There was another pause, shorter this time. "It's just…unexpected."

"Especially on a random Christmas night after all this time."

"Something like that."

"If you'd rather not talk, I understand. I just wanted to say "Hi"."

"I'm glad you did. But can I ask why?" Bill was confused but not displeased. "It's been a long time since we last spoke."

"I know. But an old friend….well, "old friend" is a bit of a generous term but she reminded me that we were inseparable at one time. I miss those days."

Bill was quiet for a moment. "I don't. We were hellions back then and I regret a lot of what we did." He paused again. "But I miss you. You were the best friend I've ever had."

Relief swept through Brice. "I miss you too. We had some great times."

"Until it all went bottoms-up."

"Yeah, sorry about all that."

"No need to apologize. I was just as much at fault. And just as stupid." Bill laughed, thinking back to all that had happened in the aftermath of their one particular poor choice. "But you know what? That's in the past. I think it's time to move forward."

"I think you're right," Brice offered. "You always were the smarter one."

"Better looking too!"

The inside joke they used to banter about between them constantly so long ago came rushing back as they both let out a hearty laugh.

"So who is this "old friend" who convinced you to get in touch with me again?" Bill couldn't imagine anyone who Brice might have run into that knew him as well.

"You remember Kelsie from school..."

They talked for over an hour, just like old friends do, even ones that were once close but hadn't spoken in years. Brice was pleased beyond words to learn of his friend's successes and family while Bill was thrilled to learn that Brice had moved back to the area. Eventually Brice looked at the clock.

"Man, I'm so sorry to have kept you on the phone so late on Christmas night. You're wife is not gonna be happy."

"Don't sweat it. She was so exhausted after the busy day we had that she went to bed right after the phone rang. I think she was happy to have an excuse to slip away."

"Please apologize to her for me. I didn't mean to take up so much of your time tonight."

"I'm glad you did. And why don't you apologize in person? Let's get together!"

"That sounds great. How about after the New Year starts? I'm heading north to ski for a few days with my niece."

"Sounds good. Call me when you get back."

"I will, if you mean it." Brice was afraid his old friend was just being polite.

"Damn right I mean it. I've got your number now so if you don't call me, I'm calling you!"

"I'll call."

"You better. Goodnight Brice. Merry Christmas."

"Goodnight Bill. It is a Merry Christmas now."

As Brice ended the call, he felt a sense of calm that had been missing in his life for quite some time. His earlier conversation with Kelsie had offered him an opportunity he didn't expect to ever present it-self. And then, with another conversation, he managed to wipe out the biggest regret he had held onto over the years. The one person he had never contacted to make things right was Bill. Yet with one phone call, all was right on Christmas night.

He smiled as he reflected on what had been his best Christmas ever.

***

Kelsie walked to the kitchen wearing a satisfied smile. After feeling her Christmas couldn't have gotten any better, her conversation with Brice had improved it even more. The mention of his New Year's plans keep replaying in her mind as Jessie walked into the kitchen and opened the fridge.

"You aren't actually hungry after the dinner I made, are you?"

He looked intently at everything on the shelves, then closed the door. "Not really. Just kinda want something. Not being able to get a decent snack for a month was tough. I guess I just want to be able to do it again."

"Understandable. And even though I didn't make a whole lot of cookies, we can finish off what we have."

Jessie smiled and reopened the refrigerator. "I'll grab the milk!"

Kelsie took the snowman cookie jar from its place on the counter and sat on a stool at the island as she removed the lid. Jessie filled two glasses with ice-cold milk and then sat next to his mother and dug his hand into the jar.

"Guess what."

Kelsie dug into the jar after him. "What?"

"You know how I've been pretty clueless about what I'm going to study in college?"

She nodded with a mouthful of cookie, surprised he was bringing up the subject she had been asking him about ever since the school year started. She knew it was a decision he had been avoiding.

"Well, I've decided what I want to do with my life."

"Straight from not even knowing what you want to study to knowing what you want to do for the rest of your life?" Kelsie was mildly shocked.

He nodded with a wide grin plastered on his face. "I've decided I want to be a vet."

"A vet?" Kelsie swallowed her last bite of cookie. "As in veterinarian, I hope."

"What other kind is there?" He winked.

Kelsie breathed a sigh of relief but wondered if he had thought his plan through. "That's quite an involved field of study. Can I ask how you came to this realization?"

"Bailey. I really liked being around him. And helping him. And I love animals. So I'd like to help as many as I can."

She contemplated his reasoning for several moments. "Sounds like the perfect choice for you."

"You really think so? I know it's not gonna be easy but I think it'll be worth it in the end."

"It sounds like you chose it for all the right reasons. You do love animals and if you do something you love..." She paused intentionally.

"...You'll never work a day in your life." Jessie broke into a wide grin as he finished his father's favorite saying.

He actually had had the dream of being a vet for a while but he never talked about. He wanted to tell his father so they could discuss the idea and debate the pros and cons. But his father was no longer there. Yet in telling his mother about his dream, he somehow felt he had also told his dad. "So you really think I can do it?"

"I'm certain you can do whatever you set your mind to. You turned your life around, didn't you?"

"Yeah, well, I hope I didn't screw things up so much that I can't get into college."

He had a point. But she had confidence in him, especially after seeing how he had changed so drastically. "You managed to not screw up your grades during all of this so I'm not worried."

"I hope you're right."

"Just focus on your dream and you'll be fine." She smiled as she starred at Jessie. "My son, the doctor."

He blushed. "You're gonna love calling me that any chance you get, aren't you?"

She reached over and tousled his hair. "You know I am!"

Jessie felt good about his choice but nervous at the same time. However, his mother's confidence in his abilities in turn bolstered his confidence. He decided then and there that nothing was going to stop him from achieving his goal. He had to keep his life moving along the right track.

"Guess what," Kelsie said as the idea that had been rolling around in her head finally jelled.

"You wanna be a vet too?" he teased.

"Since school doesn't start again until the 5th, how about we go somewhere this year to ring in the New Year?"

Jessie was a little perplexed. They had never gone anywhere for New Year's. It had always been a holiday they celebrated at home, crowds never being something any of them liked to endure. "What do you have in mind?"

Chapter Twenty

The clear skies that were present at the start of their trip north gave way to clouds threatening snow. *Perfect,* Kelsie thought as they neared their destination. The drive had taken less time than anticipated so she felt they would get some good runs in before they checked into the rooms she had reserved for her and Jessie. She was glad he had been up for the spur-of-the-moment trip but as they approached the mountain base, she became nervous. The trip had been totally impulsive, something very much out-of-character for her and there was a very good chance her hoped for result for the trip might not work out at all. She'd soon find out.

She turned into the parking lot and found it to be modest, not something that could accommodate hundreds of cars, to her relief. A small number of parked cars usually meant the slopes would not be crowded, unless busloads of skiers had been brought in. But with not a bus in sight, she glanced at the slopes facing the parking lot and found them to be dotted with skiers instead of the steady stream of people sliding down the mountain that she was used to. The last time she had skied with Jessie and his father, they couldn't get down the slopes without dodging multiple skiers and snowboarders. It hadn't been much fun. To her, Sutton looked promising.

They parked, put on their gear and purchased lift tickets in what seemed like record time. Kelsie studied the trail map and found several trails she wanted to check out. The mountain was tall enough that their runs would be nice and long, just what she was hoping for. She was so looking forward to getting on the slopes again that she almost forgot the other thing she was hoping for out of the trip.

As Jessie made his final preparations and clicked his boots into his skis, a gentle snow started to fall. He loved skiing in snow. So did Kelsie, who seemed to be spending more time looking at the snow than preparing to ski down the mountain on it. As they made their way to the lift, her eyes were scanning everyone at the base of the mountain. Jessie was getting ready to ask what she was looking for when she started waving her hands as she broke into a broad smile.

"Who are you waving to?" he asked. "You haven't been here long enough to know anybody." He had always marveled at his mother's ability to get to know people minutes after walking into a room.

Kelsie just smiled and nodded towards something that was behind him. Jessie turned around to see Brice approaching.

"Hey you two," Brice greeted them with a broad smile as he poled his way over. "Glad you made it."

Kelsie flashed an equally broad smile.

Jessie was totally perplexed. "What do you mean "glad you made it"?"

"I have a confession," Kelsie offered. "After Brice told me he was bringing his niece here for New Year's, I kinda invited us to join them."

"You mean you invited us to crash their vacation?" Jessie was embarrassed. "Not cool Mom."

"Don't give your mother a hard time," Brice interjected. "I thought it was a great idea!"

"Glad to hear it." Kelsie looked around. "Speaking of your niece, where is she?"

"She had to get her skis adjusted. She should be back any minute."

"So you planned all this Mom?"

"Well, after you told me you liked my idea to go skiing for New Year's, I called Brice and asked if we could join them."

"What if he had said "no"?"

"Then we would have still gone skiing, just not here." Kelsie blushed as she looked at Brice. "But fortunately he said "yes"."

"I gladly said "yes"," he eagerly confirmed. "If I had been brave enough, I would have invited you two before you asked."

Kelsie gave him a look. "I never knew you to be a coward about asking a girl anything."

"One of the many things that has changed about me since school," he winked. "These days I'm terrified of getting turned down."

"That wasn't going to happen." Kelsie flashed him her most earnest look.

Just as Jessie was wishing he was anywhere but there, Brice looked over his shoulder. "Here's my niece now."

Jessie turned around to see April approaching with skis slung over her shoulder. His mouth dropped open. "April is your niece?!?!"

"It's true," he stated, watching Jessie's reaction, hoping it didn't take a turn south. He knew that April never mentioned the relation. So far, Jessie just seemed surprised. He hoped that was the most intense reaction that would be forthcoming.

Kelsie stared at Brice in disbelief as April reached them.

"Hey everyone," she greeted them nonchalantly. "You made it!"

"You knew we were coming?" Kelsie wondered.

"Brice asked if I minded once you asked about joining us." She flashed Jessie an earnest smile. "Sounded fun to me."

Jessie suddenly didn't appear to be happy to see April. Or Brice. He moved away from the group, acting as though he needed space to adjust his skis. Or gloves. Or anything he could think to do that didn't involve anyone else. It was exactly what Brice had been worried might happen. He started to follow Jessie but April put her hand on his arm to hold him back. The look on her face let him know she wanted to explain things to him and, most likely, answer his uppermost questions regarding why she never told him who her uncle was.

She approached Jessie slowly as Brice and Kelsie moved away. "You OK?"

Jessie wasn't certain how he was. He felt betrayed. He knew something hadn't seemed right since he rarely saw April at Redemption after dinner. He had always figured she had things to do but now he knew that it was because she went home each night. She wasn't an "inmate", like him. She was there to...he didn't know what.

"Why didn't you tell me?" were the only words he could muster.

"I don't know," she replied. "It obviously never came up."

"Why would it?" he shot back. "Why would I have any idea that he's related to you unless you brought it up?"

"It's just not something I tell people."

"Why, so you can spy on kids in the program and then tell him what we say?" Jessie's anger at the situation was growing, evident in his intense tone.

"No," she stated emphatically. "It wasn't like that with you. I wanted to get to know you and I knew you wouldn't talk to me the way you did if you knew Brice was my uncle."

"Gee, I wonder why," Jessie replied with venomous sarcasm in his voice as his heart pounded in his chest.

"That's exactly it. You would have shut down and I truly felt that some of the talks we had were helpful to you. You seemed relieved to get things off your chest. And I felt good that I might have been helping you."

Jessie slowed his thoughts enough to start comprehending what April was saying. It was true that the reason he spoke to her about private things was because it felt good to do so. Until April came along, he had never realized he might be able to open up to a girl without feeling judged.

"But I told you stuff. Stuff that I didn't want anyone else to know!" He leaned into her and whispered intently. "Especially my counselor!"

"I know. I'm sorry I never said anything," April pleaded. "But Jessie, I swear, I didn't tell him anything you told me in confidence. I never actually told him anything, I promise."

From his vantage point, it was obvious to Brice that Jessie was not taking the news well. He approached them as he heard April's last statement. "Actually, that's not true."

April jumped when she heard his voice as it contradicted what she had told Jessie. She wheeled around and shot him a look of daggers.

"She did tell me one thing about you Jessie. She told me you were worth the work I was putting into you."

April breathed a sigh of relief as Jessie stared at her.

"Why?" he asked.

April gave him a look that said *don't be stupid.* When he responded with the same expression, she blurted it out. "Because you are, you idiot! I could tell there's a good, solid person in you. I haven't had training like Brice but I've got intuition. I can tell when someone in the program has potential or just isn't going to get it. And I knew you were going to get it! And I wanted to make sure that Brice knew you were going to get it!"

Brice finally interjected. "It's true Jessie. She knew you were struggling and she knew I was struggling to help you. But the only thing I could get out of her was that she thought you were capable of something special. And I'm thinking she's probably right."

Jessie was quiet for a moment, then looked squarely at Brice. "Even if I was worth the extra work, I'm probably not the type of guy you'd want dating your niece." He was suddenly embarrassed. He had never mentioned anything about dating to April but he had thought about her a lot since leaving Redemption and was hoping they might continue spending time together. But he never intended to toss his feelings out so forwardly, especially to a group that included his mother and his counselor.

Brice carefully considered his response before offering it. He finally looked at Jessie squarely. "Why wouldn't I? Everyone deserves to find love...eventually." He glanced over at Kelsie and winked.

Kelsie overheard as she approached. "I whole-heartedly agree!"

"Don't I get a say in this?" April interjected. "He hasn't even officially asked me out on a date and you're throwing the L-word around!" She looked at Jessie hoping to see a softening attitude.

"You gonna tell him what we do on our date...if we ever have one?" Jessie replied sarcastically.

April was relieved his sense of humor had returned. It was one of the many things she liked about him.

Brice put his fingers in his ears and laughed. "I don't want to know anything about what my niece does with her boyfriend."

"Again, I need to remind everyone," April quickly interjected, "we haven't even gone on a date yet and you're already calling him my boyfriend!"

Kelsie joined in. "Trust me, I can already see where this is going."

Jessie feigned severe embarrassment. "Mom!"

As Brice and Kelsie moved away, wanting to give them some space, April moved closer to Jessie, nudging his shoulder with hers. The smile that came across his face brought her great relief. "You can kiss me if you want." She wasn't sure why the words spilled from her mouth so easily but they were certainly true.

"Before our first date?"

"Why not?"

So there, at the base of the mountain, in the falling snow, and with his mother in closer proximity than Jessie had ever imagined she would be when he had his first kiss, it happened. April's lips felt soft on his and though he would never admit it to anyone, his heart skipped a beat.

He debated in his head whether or not he should try for another kiss. But before he could decide if it was OK or not, April went for it.

And his heart skipped another beat.

***

Kelsie and Brice watched the young couple from a distance, wanting them to feel a little less self conscious.

"I'm thinking he might get over this little surprise," Kelsie remarked as she watched her son kiss Brice's niece for the third time.

"You may just be right," Brice agreed. "And I have to say, they are inspiring."

Kelsie looked at him with a quizzical, yet hopeful look in her eyes.

"I'm hoping that you can finally get over the past and give me a proper chance." He matched her hopeful stare.

She blushed. "I think I've finally realized that the past is in the past. All of it. Far in the past. Otherwise, I wouldn't be here."

"I'm really glad to hear that. It'll make things less awkward in a moment."

She had no idea what he was talking about. Then, out of the blue, he leaned over and kissed her. She tried to act surprised but she was actually relieved.

And happy.

And she had that tingling feeling she hadn't felt for a long, long time.

He felt odd too. He realized as their kiss ended that he was experiencing a feeling he had never previously felt. He liked it.

Finally, Kelsie spoke. "That was very nice."

Brice blushed as he responded. "Yes, it was. Is that what it feels like at the end of a third date?" The smile he beamed at her was so intense he felt as though his face might break

"I'd say it's something very much like that."

"Cool. Wonder what a fourth date feels like."

"Stick around and find out."

"Oh, I intend to do just that." He held her close for several moments. "Ready to hit the slopes?"

"In a minute," Kelsie responded, just before she kissed him again.

THE END

MICHAEL J. MOORE started writing after years of working in the music and movie distribution business. The change in direction started with his work as Co-Producer and Music Supervisor for the film *Day Of The Gun* featuring Eric Roberts. He then appeared as Reverend Robert Lowe in the feature film *Bill Tilghman and the Outlaws,* which led to him writing and acting in three short inspirational/western films exploring the Lowe character's back story. At his wife's suggestion, he turned those scripts into his first short-story collection, *The Tales Of Robert Lowe,* which was followed by a prequel book, *Robert Lowe: An Origin Story.* His third book, the first in a planned series of novels inspired by his mother's love of holiday films, was *A Cowboy Christmas.* Here he continues his holiday book series with another heart-warming story. A life-long resident of Maryland, he and his wife now live in South Carolina.